Which is the Real Ramon?

S. GILL WILLIAMSON

DEDICATION

This story is dedicated to the author's mentor, Santa Barbara amateur astronomer Leland S. Copeland, and to the natural historians of his "Lost Galaxy" NGC 4535 of the Virgo Cluster. We will never know what they have discovered..

CONTENTS

INTRODUCTION

Humans are fascinated by stories of intergalactic travel where people beam down to strange worlds and travel faster than the speed of light to get there. But biological humans are fragile and have evolved over millions of years to live on earth. This story explores the way such intergalactic adventures can actually take place, provided only that humans expand their notion of self. Advances in computer science such as virtual reality and synthetic intelligence will make it possible to create copies of humans and provide simulated environments for these copies. These simulated or virtual humans will be able to control time and live for millions of years while traveling throughout our galaxy. In our story, the biological humans copied in this way feel disappointed with this arrangement. Their copies have all of the adventures while they, the biological humans, die in the usual way by growing old. Our story describes motivations and technologies that gradually result in the biological humans identifying with their virtual copies in a way that connects their sense of self with their copies and the more advanced civilization that maintains the copies.

1 AMANDA

The Picnic: July 2060

Stacks of plates sat on tables. Ice chests of cold drinks dotted the lawn. Technicians from ERVS swarmed about the perimeter of the picnic area. Motes were scattered everywhere, archiving the event for history.

Amanda joined the guests queuing for last-minute bio-checks. She looked out at the happy gathering of friends and relatives all of them unaware of the advanced technology that was violating their privacy. She waved to her parents in the distance. Their thirtieth anniversary -- her attendance was required.

"You're crazy to let ERVS do this, Mom," she had warned. "The personal avatars they create aren't just toys that look and act like us, they're living beings."

As a graduate student at Berkeley, Amanda participated in an ERVS Turing test. She conducted an online interview, first with Ramon(A) and then with Ramon(B). One was a physics graduate student, her boyfriend; the other was an ERVS personal avatar, a virtual copy of Ramon. She was to identify which is the real Ramon.

At the end of the sessions, Amanda guessed that Ramon(A) was her boyfriend. She was wrong.

Now, after her first year as an assistant professor of computer science at CMU, she knew much more about ERVS and its innovative technology. What she knew troubled her. ERVS computer scientists, programmers and systems engineers were masterful technicians, but they lived in narrow worlds. The top managers, clever and intelligent, conveniently ignored the potential for evil that they were overseeing.

An ERVS technician shoved a small bio-identification device in front of Amanda's face and squinted at the tiny screen. "Welcome to the picnic, Amanda Stever. Your virtual copy has been programmed. Please pick your spot on the grounds."

People stood in small groups. Their personal avatars in the ERVS virtual version of the picnic would be in the same positions and would have the same past memories and expectations for the afternoon as their human counterparts. Descendents of people at the real picnic would, using ERVS immersion equipment, be able to attend replays of the virtual picnic for a price. To maximize profit ERVS would randomly initiate each replay. Each session, starting off slightly different from the others, would evolve into new experiences and conversations.

But that was the optimistic scenario.... Existing virtual reality platforms, much less sophisticated than those of ERVS, were already selling sadistic thrill experiences. Amanda decided to take action to protect her personal avatar.

"Hi guys," Amanda said, approaching her cousin, Harvey, who stood surrounded by his college friends. She forced her way to the center of their group. "See that table to the right of the grandstand? I want all of you to walk over there with me before the recording session starts." She grabbed the shirts of the guys on either side of her and nudged them forward. Harvey and his friends shuffled ahead, sheltering Amanda from view.

"Stop," she said. "Stand here for a moment while I get under the table. Then disperse slowly. Don't tell anyone where I am or I'll hunt you down and kill you." She was only half joking. She quickly ducked under the table as the bell for the start of the session sounded.

The table, covered to the ground with a large dark cloth and holding a pair of speakers, sat against a small grandstand. It would be a deafening afternoon for Amanda.

ERVS: April 2140

An immense building, four stories above ground and three below, sat on a coastal terrace north of UC San Diego. It contained the most sophisticated computers in the world. Above the main entrance were the words EVENT

RETRIEVAL AND VIRTUAL SIMULATION. Known worldwide as ERVS, it was the leading company in virtual reality based simulation.

An elderly man, tall with grey hair, entered the building and approached an elevator, its door held open by a young engineer.

"Hi Sandman! What's new?" the engineer asked with a smile.

Errett Castillo, a senior scientist in the Mote Lab, took plenty of crap. The millimeter diameter smartdust or motes, derisively called "sand" by the simulation engineers, were tasked with creating the ERVS archival event records.

"The sand is getting smarter every day," Errett joked. "Some emergent behavior is evident. Be careful shaking out your hiking boots." There was no reply.

In his office, Errett checked his calendar. Nothing for three weeks. Management counted on the motes for accurate background and archival recording, but as long as Errett's motes were keeping up with innovations on the virtual reality side, he and his group were left alone. He grabbed some coffee and headed for the Mote Lab to check on his senior test engineer.

"Hola, Laura!" Errett said as he entered, looking for a place to sit down in the mess. Overlapping posters announcing political events past and future papered the walls. Stacks of newsletters turned the room into a jumbled maze. Laura was taking risks with political advocacy in her office, but she was brilliant at testing motes and predicting problems.

"Want to see something interesting? Look at these clusters." Laura pointed to a flat silicon surface covered by a small clear plastic dome. Three small groups of motes, chilled to well below zero, sat close together. "Each mote hosts a human avatar."

Errett froze in disbelief. "What are you doing, Laura? These motes don't have the computational power to host a human. If you've messed with their CPUs we're in big trouble."

"I haven't messed with the CPUs. Have you checked the specs on these new motes? They're unbelievable. Each one has the power to host a virtual human plus a small but pleasant work environment."

In haste, he had approved use of these new motes without studying their specs. A big mistake it now seemed. He stood in silence, looking at the three clusters.

"If management finds out about this, you and I are in big trouble," he said.

"The company we work for has become a criminal enterprise," Laura said, jumping to her feet and starting to pace around the room. "These guys are making money selling virtual murder, rape and pedophilia."

Errett had heard all of this before. By going outside her need-to-know security domain, Laura had recorded many instances where ERVS clients had committed terrible acts while immersed in event simulations -- things that would be serious crimes if committed against real people instead of virtual people.

"At the end of each simulation everything is essentially reinitialized to the original event. The avatars remember nothing about what happened during the immersion," Errett said, repeating the official line.

"Sure they're reset," Laura replied. "But the avatars are alive, they feel pain and humiliation."

"Right. It's a moral issue, but you're dealing with some very powerful people. How many humans have you downloaded to the sand?"

"Hundreds. Many more to follow," Laura said, standing and facing Errett. "Sit down, relax. I'll explain what's going on and needs to be done."

Daggett: May 2140

Team leader Daggett settled into his TIS (Total Immersion Systems) couch to finalize hookup; the two other members of his team were doing the same. In this game, ironically called "Amanda's Picnic," they had failed in the first two sessions. They had not even managed to locate their intended victim. After each failed session, ERVS would choose an initialization setting that made their task harder. No other team had been able to locate Amanda in the first two sessions either. Those few that went on to the third session all failed. ERVS kept the details of failed sessions secret.

Daggett's team could quit now and minimize their losses, but if they succeeded in the third try it would enhance their reputation in the gaming society. They voted to go for the third try.

Their team's gaming specialty was rape. According to the rules, they had be immersed in an ERVS sponsored simulation, lure their target to a hidden place and take turns with her. Their avatars had to survive the encounter, and the victim had to be a functioning avatar when their team was extracted from the scene. The challenge was to avoid being attacked by the other avatars at the assigned event.

Amanda's Picnic was unique. Daggett had studied the ERVS sample simulations with an experienced eye. The assigned victim, Amanda, was on the original list of attendees but had never appeared in the game initializations. She had to be there somewhere, but where?

There were only three possible hiding places for Amanda: under the grandstand or under one of the two speaker tables. Checking under the grandstand had been time consuming and ended the team's first immersion. In the second immersion, they verified she was not under the speaker table to the left of the grandstand. Only the speaker table to the right of the grandstand remained as a possible hiding place. If there, she would be trapped, and they could take her one at a time, her screams hidden by the blaring music.

Now in deep immersion under the control of TIS computers linked to those of ERVS, the avatars of Daggett and his two team members stood together at the edge of the picnic grounds. They looked across the lawn at the speaker table. Some college boys were standing nearby, but no Amanda in sight. The three virtual visitors slowly worked their way in the direction of the table.

Amanda Arrives: July 2140

Alarmed by the silence, Amanda listened, parted the cloth, and peeked out at a vast lawn. A small group of people approached the table. They began to shout and applaud.

"It's Amanda!" someone yelled, "She made it safely." A young woman approached, smiled, and offered her hand.

"Welcome, Amanda," she said, motioning to the others to gather round. "We're all admirers of your work and pleased to have you join our group."

Amanda looked them over -- all strangers. What were they talking about? Her only work was her Ph.D. dissertation and related papers. She tried to speak, was interrupted by more applause, and then managed to get some words out.

"Thank you, but where are my parents and the rest of the guests?"

A young man stepped forward. "Your parents and the rest are fine," he said. "Dead, but fine."

Amanda gasped and held tightly to the table. "Dead?"

The young woman approached and put her arm around Amanda's shoulder.

"I am so sorry," she said, in a soothing voice. "Kevin is a great computer scientist, but he's terribly blunt. Your bio-parents lived long and productive lives and died of old age. This is July 15, 2140. You crawled under the table eighty years ago."

Amanda took a few steps back from the group and looked around in wonder.

"Silence everyone! This isn't how we planned to greet Amanda," the elderly man said, introducing himself as Errett. "Come with us, Amanda, we have a small reception with food and drink waiting. It's in the building across the lawn." Amanda looked at the Spanish style building wondering why she hadn't noticed it before.

"We've duplicated the fried chicken and potato salad from your picnic -- dishes that were served while you were under the table," Errett said, as they arrived at an outdoor patio buffet.

Amanda gratefully accepted some lemonade and worked her way through the admiring crowd to where the blunt speaking Kevin stood alone. "What's going on, Kevin?" she asked. "You don't mince words."

"Think of yourself as Amanda(A)." Kevin said, with a mischievous grin.

Amanda got it. She looked at the beautiful blue sky and her half empty glass of lemonade. It tasted great. "So this is a simulation," she said. "It all seems so real. Ramon(B) is probably dead, but what happened to Ramon(A)? Not that I want to see him."

"Dragged to the trash long ago. He was an even older version than you."

Amanda was concerned. "I seem to be just as functional as the rest of these folks," she said. "Am I out of date?"

"You're not out of date as an avatar. The process of extracting you from the picnic simulation automatically updated your data structures to modern standards. You're our oldest successful extraction."

"Was I copied or extracted? " Amanda asked, realizing that she was a virtual being and the question was relevant.

"Copied is better. The original Amanda still has a personal avatar at the picnic under the table. That virtual Amanda, your original copy, is now in great danger."

"What sort of danger?" Amanda asked.

"The Immersion Rights Party got control of the government about ten years ago after the election of President Tannenbaum. That was the start of widespread abuse of avatars by groups of gamers. Several gamer teams, rapists, have fixated on you, Amanda. Search engines show you were at the picnic, but your original virtual self has never been seen in any simulation. That fascinates them."

"So as long as they fail to locate me, the other guests are safe?"

"The gamers are now convinced your original version is under the table in the simulation they are working with. The avatars of your cousin Harvey and two of his friends were injured defending your table during the group's third attack. That virtual Harvey might be killed next time if he gets in the way."

Amanda knew that the simulation would be reset each time the gamers attacked. Poor virtual Harvey would have learned nothing from the previous attacks while the gamers would remember every detail. It was a cruel business, unfair to the avatars.

"Why do people now living ever allow ERVS to record them?" Amanda asked Kevin.

"All simulated events in the last decade are supposed to be stored in secure archives. ERVS agreed to not allow gamers at them," Kevin replied.

"Until the price is right," Amanda said, frowning with anger. "So these Immersion Rights creeps have opened all simulations done prior to their coming to power for exploitation."

"You're a quick learner and a leader, Amanda. That's why you're here."

"People in this century must be even dumber than those in the twenty-first century," Amanda thought to herself. "Not a good sign."

Errell approached them. "I'll show you to your casita, Amanda, so you can be alone and get some rest. In the morning, we will have breakfast together and talk." Motioning Amanda to follow, he started across the lawn toward a small adobe building surrounded by a pebbled cactus garden.

Alone and in pleasant settings, Amanda began to think about her situation. She thought about her biological parents. Her memories of their lives were now much more detailed than those of her original biological self. Other thoughts and memories were also greatly enhanced. She had an increased awareness of her physical body. She was aware of a deep and more sophisticated knowledge of computer science. Exhausted she curled up on her bed and fell asleep.

Amanda's New Home: July 2140

Amanda awoke to the increasing light, got dressed, and walked barefoot across the smooth tiles to the window of her small room. She watched as the lawn and building of yesterday's festivities reappeared in stages. When the scene was complete, she saw Kevin and Errett walking across the lawn toward her casita. She put two extra mugs next to the coffee pot and propped the door open. Kevin, followed by Errett, entered.

"Good morning, Amanda," Kevin said. "Sorry about not getting the building and lawn back fast enough. We couldn't launch the scene until we docked our motes, and then we had some problems of our own doing. We're still learning."

"OK guys, what's going on?" Amanda asked, sipping her coffee.

Kevin walked to the other side of the room and through a narrow door. "This room is where you control your mote, Amanda. It is a physical object in what we call the "bio world." A large central screen showed three tank-like ellipsoidal shapes huddled spoke-like on a black surface. Appendages appeared from their sides.

"Meet the sources of our physical existence, Amanda," Errett said. "One mote for each of us."

"They look like water bears," Amanda said, remembering her biology class.

"They're about the same size and are on a chilled cryo plate," Errett said.

Amanda got the idea. "So my mote alone can simulate me and my local environment. The lawn and building requires all three of our motes linked together. Fascinating! Alone in my casita, I exist in my mote's computer. Now I exist in the combined resources of all three of our motes."

"The fiesta yesterday required the combined resources of all attendees linked together in Laura's lab," Errett added.

Amanda knew she was a virtual being, a greatly enhanced personal avatar of the long-dead bio-Amanda. She and her mote together constituted a real, physical being in the year 2140. She felt a sense of power.

ERVS: July 2140

The "biological" Errett, as he had come to think of himself, entered Laura's lab and shut the door. Laura sat huddled over the microscope.

"I separated these three motes from the rest. Now they've docked on their own," Laura announced.

"I suppose the virtual Errett's mote is one of them," Errett said. "You like to experiment with him."

"Your mote is one, Kevin's is the second. Amanda's mote is the third, but she doesn't know how to control anything at this point."

Errett sat down and looked in the microscope. "Now they're undocking, one mote is moving backwards" he remarked with indifference

Laura pushed Errett aside. "That's Amanda's mote. They must be giving her lessons. That's great!"

Errett knew that Laura's avatars and their corresponding motes were becoming independent of her. When the motes physically moved in real space, they could be observed with the proper equipment. But when they were linked together in a wireless network, they controlled their own simulated worlds.

"The one thing that unites these enhanced human avatars is their hatred of the gamers," Laura said. "I have programmed Amanda's mote so she can hack into the ERVS programs that run simulations for the gamers. Let's see what she can do!"

"We're not going to have much say about her strategy," Errett whispered to himself.

The Fourth Try, TIS: October 2140

On Daggett's third attempt, the avatars of Harvey and his friends had attacked their team's avatars as they neared the table on the right of the grandstand; Daggett's team was now certain of Amanda's hiding place. This knowledge alone would increase their reputation as gamers. They could stop at three attempts. His team could still gain some points for publishing Amanda's hiding place on their blog. Other gamers could have a shot at her on their first try.

On the other hand, risking a rare fourth try with an initialization difficulty of 9 or 10, and successfully carrying it off, would get them important recognition among the best gamers. President Tannenbaum, himself a gamer, would invite them to the White House.

TIS technicians, scantily clad female med techs, welcomed them as they moved to the immersion couches. The meticulous hookup took twenty minutes. A barely audible buzzer sounded and the three men drifted under.

Now at the virtual picnic, Daggett's avatar clutched his small stun gun. His team would lose points if they had to stun Harvey; finesse mattered. The avatars of Harvey and his friends stood near Amanda's table just like in the last game. But luckily this time, distracted by an attractive young woman waving to them from the edge of the picnic grounds, started to move in her direction.

Daggett's avatar stood still for a few minutes, sensed the time was right, nodded to his teammates, and started toward the table. Suddenly, he stopped and looked down. He reached between his legs, felt around, gasped, doubled over, and fell to the ground. His teammates, leaderless and terrified, froze.

At TIS, Dr. Mendoza was the first to reach the writhing, semi-conscious Daggett. She called for help. A large technician arrived in seconds and pulled back Daggett's arms and hands, forcing them away from his crotch. He pulled back the sheet that had been placed over Daggett's lower body. Everything seemed intact.

Daggett was going into shock. The sensors in his groin had unexpectedly recorded intense pain.

The TIS supervisor arrived at the scene. "If any of you breathe a word of this, you're fired," he yelled at the med techs. "Get these other two guys out of immersion and keep them occupied while we get Daggett straightened out."

Dr. Mendoza remained silent. She had never seen anything like this. How would TIS cover up such a mess? The other team members, less traumatized than Daggett, would remember their virtual experiences and surely tell what happened -- unless they were too embarrassed to reveal the details of yet another failure.

Meanwhile, Laura had watched the TIS immersion and Daggett's fourth try using her hacked links to the ERVS simulators. She had penetrated ERVS security but not the TIS computers or event recorders. The ERVS side was enough to alarm her -- she knew immediately what had happened and who was responsible.

Errett heard Laura shouting in frustration as he entered the lab. "Amanda could have cut off anything else," she cried. "A finger, an ear, a toe, that would have been bad enough. Daggett needed his index finger to fire the stun gun. Why not cut that off? Why this? This will trigger a full ERVS investigation."

Errett tried to calm her. "These gamers would die a horrible death before complaining about this to ERVS. Their macho egos will keep them silent. As for TIS management, they're scared to death. If this gets out, other gamers won't come near the TIS salon out of fear of the same mutilation.

"Maybe you're right," Laura said. "Amanda can't get away with this more than once.

"Have virtual Laura get together with Amanda in a training session and talk some sense into her while you still have some control over this," Errett said.

"I've lost control of virtual Laura," she said, with more relief than sadness.

"You've definitely lost control of Amanda! You endowed her with way too much information about the ERVS system design and code during her enhancement phase. You've created a monster."

Laura was afraid for herself and her colleagues at ERVS. She thought of the brutal prison camps and interrogation centers of the Tannenbaum administration.

"Let's hope Amanda's desire for revenge has been satisfied. Hope is all we can do now," she whispered. She was afraid to admit to Errett her personal attachment to Amanda and the actual degree to which she had enhanced her data structures with detailed information about the ERVS system.

The Journey Begins: January 2141

Errett sat in his office where he had spent New Year's Eve alone. He had been drinking. Amazingly, neither he nor Laura had been fired. In fact, ERVS and the world were still clueless about what was happening.

His first fateful decision came last March when he approved converting all of the motes to the newest model with their greatly improved repair kits. These kits were miniature fabrication factories capable of repairing or manufacturing new motes and new fabrication factories under any field conditions. Initially under Laura's supervision and then on their own, the motes with their virtual human hosts learned to operate these fab factories.

After virtual Amanda's dramatic castration of Daggett's personal avatar, she changed her approach to the less dramatic. Only minor "Immersion Trouble Reports," or ITR's as they came to be called, occurred during gaming sessions: a shoe missing, no pants or shirt, slightly odd skin coloration, memory impairment, etc. The accepted explanation for these minor abnormalities was that the legacy systems used by the gaming salons needed replacement. Minor ITR's, however, were enough to bring immediate attention to gamers as they immersed themselves in sessions. They were quickly recognized as intruders and countered by the event's avatars.

The news of the evening reported that an automated unmanned cargo ship bound for Mars had mysteriously veered off course going out of the ecliptic at a steep angle. The ship carried thousands of new motes and a large supply of the latest fab factories. Unknown to authorities, hundreds of human-based motes with all the equipment they needed to make thousands more motes similarly hosted were headed somewhere. Errett and Laura had risked their careers faking records to set these events in motion, but they had left the destination decision up to virtual Amanda and Kevin.

Most likely, the ship would avoid all interplanetary traffic and probably end up on some minor planet or asteroid with a high-inclination orbit. There they would have cold operating environments for their computers with enough matter and energy to sustain them indefinitely.

Errett finished his wine and poured another glass to welcome the new year. He was fading. He felt jealous of the virtual Erretts. They and their evolving civilization would have almost eternal life. They could travel the galaxy without concern for the passage of time.

They would have the resources to improve their motes and learn how to assemble them into functional structures for different tasks. They could live near the center of the galaxy or in the outer reaches. All they would need is matter and energy under a wide range of conditions -- very different from the limited possibilities for bio-human habitats in space. But he also saw problems. The increasingly sophisticated motes might themselves become sentient synthetic life forms. Would these evolved life forms continue to host the humans?

What would be the purpose of their civilization? They would need a purpose.
The study of the natural history of the galaxy, its evolving life forms and their
struggles to survive, would be complex enough to occupy the talents of the mote
civilization for the long haul. Such a purpose might dispose them to tolerate
their virtual human hosts, even feel a sense of responsibility for them. In fact,
they might end up also hosting other life forms that they discover in their travels.

If this natural history concept of purpose occurred to him, it would also occur to
the many virtual Erretts. Comforted by this thought, he fell into a sound sleep.

2 MATTHEW CASE

September 1, 2141

Small stones driven forward by a surprise rogue wave pounded against Matthew's ankles. The retreating water from the same wave drove him in a series of forced jumps ten meters farther out to sea. He turned sideways, dug his shoes into the sand, and braced himself just in time to absorb the force of a second large wave that caught him squarely on the chest, soaking his clothes, leaving saltwater and the gritty taste of sand in his mouth.

Back on dry sand he stopped to catch his breath. On the beach in front of him was a gray igneous rock about the size of a baseball. He picked it up, brushed off the sand, and put it in his pocket. He then began the long climb from the beach to his office at the top of the cliffs.

Halfway up the trail, comforted by the warmth of the midday sun, he stopped and looked back at the beach below. Large turbulent surf broke against a strong offshore wind. Translucent veils of spray arched seaward from the crests of the waves; a beautiful easily accessible beach.

In his office, he removed his wet shoes and socks and sat back to ponder his research projects in robotics and geophysics. A job in San Diego at the Scripps Institution of Oceanography, long just a dream, had become a reality. He surveyed his unopened boxes of computer equipment. It would be publish or perish at SIO. It was Friday; he had survived his first week.

Overwhelmed by the multitude of tasks facing a beginning assistant professor, his mind wandered. He thought about Linda Nguyen, a young technician in charge of the mineralogy lab. His first attempt to strike up a conversation with her went nowhere.

He examined the beach rock. About one-fourth of the specimen was a dark course grained gabbro. The remaining three-fourths was a fine grained gray diorite. He placed the rock into the large, empty drawer of his desk. Maybe analyzing this rock was an appropriate task for Linda's lab and a way for them to get acquainted. He looked up her number and called her.

"Mineralogy Lab, Linda speaking," she answered.

"Hello Linda, this is Matthew Case. We met yesterday. Remember?"

"Yes, I remember," she replied, with little enthusiasm.

"I have a rock sample that I found this morning on the beach. It's an unusual mixture of gabbro and diorite. I'd like to get some thin-sections perpendicular to the gabbro-diorite boundary."

"How big is it? Linda asked."

"I carried it up from the beach in my pocket. Can I bring it down to you?"

"I'm going to the library. I'll come by your office on the way back -- about twenty minutes."

He had enough time to go to the restroom, brush the sand out of his damp shirt and pants, and wash up a bit. He got back to his office shortly before Linda arrived.

"Nice office," she said, standing at the open door and surveying the mess. "Have you found a house big enough for you and your family?"

"I'm single," Matthew said. "I rented an apartment, walking distance from the beach." He wanted to learn more about Linda, but she had other ideas.

"So where's the sample? she asked."

He reached into the partly open desk drawer, felt for the rock, paused, opened the drawer wider and looked in. Lying on its side at the bottom of the drawer was a ceramic mug. He placed it on his desk and stared at it.

"It's certainly unusual," Linda said, with a smile. "It looks like a mug!"

Matthew had never seen the mug before. It had thick, sturdy sides – designed more for pencils than coffee.

Linda grew restless as Matthew searched frantically for his missing rock. "It's all right -- you'll find it," she said, backing out of his office.

Tired of the futile search, Matthew put his head down on his desk to rest. He awoke later with a splitting headache. The mug was gone, replaced by the beach rock, now all diorite. A small glowing rectangle displayed text on his desk.

Sorry about the mug, Professor Case, but we can't be thin-sectioned. We need to make contact with you. Speak and we will answer on the display.

Shocked and feeling beaten, he whispered, "Who are you?"

The text on the display changed .

Natural History Colony 8945UM53. We came originally from a star system in the Sagittarius Arm of this galaxy.

"Welcome to earth," he said, speaking a little louder this time. It sounded corny, but he couldn't think of anything better.

Thanks, but you are a bit late. We have been here for over 150,000,000 years. Let us have the privilege of welcoming you to earth.

Matthew's instinct was to continue the discussion and to resolve the "we" part first. "What do you mean by 'we'?" he asked.

This object you refer to as your rock sample is a complex colony of microrobotic life forms. You may refer to us as "microbots." We control computing and communication resources. We can change our shape and physical properties in many ways.

Matthew's curiosity over technical matters now excluded all other concerns, including the possibility that this was a hoax. "How many colonies like yours are here on earth?" he asked.

Over five billion natural history colonies are on earth. Working together, we control a large number of deployed sensors of all sizes. Some are mobile and some are fixed and many play a supporting repair and resupply role.

"Why are you here?" Matthew asked.

We are recording in detail the natural history of the earth, Our records include sentient virtual copies of all species and virtual simulations of their habitats and interactions.

They started monitoring the earth near the beginning of the Cretaceous Period. The virtual reality simulations would be fascinating.

"Could I see these virtual simulations?" he asked. The answer to his question was evasive.

Two summers ago, when you were in the hospital, one of our colonies made a sentient virtual copy of you which we periodically update. The most recent update was when you slept in your office after Ms. Nguyen's departure.

While installing sensors in the Los Padres National Forest, north of Santa Barbara, he volunteered to help fight a fire and had to be evacuated. He spent one day in intensive care and three more recovering from smoke inhalation and minor burns.

"You refer to my virtual copy as sentient. What do you mean by that?"

You, Matthew, are a creature of information. All of the reality you perceive is captured by your senses and interpreted in your brain. We can simulate the function of your senses and brain completely. This simulated entity can be hosted by a single microbot. Many microbots in different colonies will host you.

"Will I be updated periodically?"

We will update the virtual Matthews frequently as long as you, the biological Matthew, live. The virtual Matthews will be able to relive, in virtual environments, experiences from your natural life. They will also have adventures of their own choosing to experience long after you are dead. You will have almost eternal life.

Matthew had sometimes made fun of the religious notions of eternal life. How ironic that this weird form of eternal life was now his. The being he thinks of as himself would expire by one of the usual methods while his virtual selves will have amazing adventures long after his death.

"May I inform other humans about you and your mission on earth?"

If you attempt to inform others, no harm will come to you other than a certain loss of face. We will erase all memories of your contacts with us from your mind, making it impossible for anyone to quiz you further about our presence.

This threat seemed very real to Matthew. The power of this strange alien civilization began to sink in.

"Why are you communicating with me?

Since our arrival on earth, we have not made our presence known. That must now change. To start with, we ask that you contact Laura Stever. She is a test engineer in the Mote Lab at ERVS just north of campus. Laura was an undergraduate at Berkeley with you. Virtual Matthew informs us that you had a computer algorithms class and a course in philosophy of religion with her.

He remembered the computer science class. He was good at the theory and bad at the programming. Laura was good at both and helped him on several assignments. He hated the philosophy of religion class.

"Why me and why Laura?"

Laura has done something that forces us to make ourselves known to her soon. She thinks highly of you and will welcome your help. We, in turn, need the help of both of you.

Laura was kind and helpful to him at Berkeley. He hadn't seen her since. Why is she being singled out by the microbots? ERVS stood for Event Recording and Virtual Reality. This alien civilization was a vast improvement on ERVS.

He would contact ERVS to see if he could get in touch with Laura

3 LAURA STEVER

September 7, 2141

At the campus food court, Matthew ordered a large house coffee. He sat down at an empty table outside on the patio, shaded from the September afternoon sun. Staring at his cup, he thought about the strange events of last Friday. He saw someone approaching. Laura smiled at him and recalled his message to her at ERVS.

"I do remember you, Matthew, and I remember the computer algorithms course." she said, as she sat down. "I'm glad I was a help to you. I'm afraid I wasn't any help to you in the philosophy course!"

"That wasn't my favorite class," Matthew said, hoping she would forget he had brought that up.

"What brings you to UC San Diego?" she asked.

"I'm an Assistant Professor of Geophysics, just started last week. My office is at SIO."

"What a beautiful place to have an office. You were on the swim team at Berkeley. Do you still swim?"

"I like to surf, especially bodysurfing, but I'm out of shape now."

"What have you been doing since Berkeley?"

"I've been in graduate school at Caltech. Remote sensors, geophysics, seismology, lots of sedentary stuff."

"Geophysics sounds fascinating. You must be a world traveler."

"There's some of that, placing sensors on various parts of the earth. What about you, Laura? What have you been up to?"

"I got my MS in computer science and was broke. I got a job at ERVS and have been there ever since. Why did you ask to see me?"

He had no idea of the extent of her knowledge about the aliens, but she must know something or they wouldn't have sent him to her. Best to be cautious. "Has anything … strange happened to you recently?" he asked. "I mean really strange?"

Laura looked down at the table. She seemed to be searching for words. "I suppose you wouldn't ask that if something strange hadn't happened to you. You brought it up, you go first."

Laura excused herself to get some coffee, giving Matthew a few minutes to compose his thoughts. When she returned, he told her about discovering the rock and about what had happened in his office.

"That's an amazing story," Laura said. "My first assumption should be that you've lost your mind." Silent for a moment, she added, "Something strange *has* happened to me recently. But it's not the same sort of thing."

"Tell me about it, and let me be the judge," Matthew said.

"I often go to the campus library on weekends. This summer an older man, well dressed, often sat at one of the tables near me. He had stacks of books but rarely looked at any of them. I tried to talk with him. He's strange, remarkable even -- but nothing as strange as your rock."

"Tell me more about him," he said. "This guy may be the reason the microbots sent me to you."

"He's a genius at history -- a favorite subject of mine. He seems to know everything in great detail. Too great. I can't verify most of the things he says, but I can't disprove them either."

"Does he tell you how he knows these things?"

"He says -- this is crazy -- he says that he has access to detailed records of everything that happened."

"The natural history colony in my office claims to have been around during all of human history," Matthew noted. "This guy may be hooked up to them."

"Sometimes he sits very still, silent for long periods, almost motionless," Laura said, looking towards the library. But other times he's talkative. When I asked him for his name, he gave me several and said I could choose one. Weird."

Weird was an understatement, Matthew thought. "Which name did you choose?"

"Valentinus," she answered. "There's a man named Valentinus that I have been reading about this summer, an important guy. He almost became the Bishop of Rome."

"Does Valentinus know things about you, surprising things?" he asked. "I think the microbots have a copy of you also."

"He does seem to know things about me that I've never told him," Laura said. "But he wouldn't need a virtual copy. He could ask around."

"For such a strange guy, asking around might be awkward," Matthew said. "He could have a device that allows him to remain in contact with the natural history colonies. Maybe it's embedded in his ear or brain."

Laura frowned. "I'm getting frightened about this, Matthew. Your imagination's running amuck."

He did have an overactive imagination, made worse by recent events -- events that stripped away the usual constraints imposed by reality. He downed the last of his coffee and took a couple of deep breaths. "I hope I'm wrong, but we must assume I'm right and think through the implications. A worst-case scenario."

"We should tell someone about this," Laura said. "We may need help."

Matthew lowered his voice. "I don't think we should tell anyone. It's the brain-erasing bit. Have you told someone other than me about Valentinus and how strange he is?"

"I've mentioned him a few times. Said I'd met a strange, slightly crazy man in the library who knew a lot of history. But no one was interested in that."

"This is the opposite of what you see in the movies," Matthew said. "These aliens have wrapped the world in a web of information. They don't want to interfere with the objects of their studies.”

“The phrase ‘web of information’ scares me,” Laura said. “Why would they be here recording everything?”

“I’m not sure,” Matthew replied. “They’re probably not after territory or extra resources. The microbots could get their energy from light, chemicals, or atomic power on a small scale. I think these microbots, for some mysterious reason, *enjoy* observing natural evolution in progress. If that’s true, the human race may be in trouble.”

“Why in trouble, if the aliens just want to observe?” Laura asked.

“Despite our best efforts we're slowly destroying the biosphere with global warming. To get the biosphere back on track maybe they will destroy the human race to reset the clock in evolutionary terms and continue entertaining themselves with the fantastic and complex struggle of life to survive.”

Laura shook her head in disagreement. “I don’t think so. They wouldn’t need our help with that.”

Matthew could see that she wasn’t going to put up with trivial conjectures. He needed more information.

“Can I meet Valentinus and talk to him? I think it’s necessary if we’re to get to the bottom of this.”

She appeared reluctant as she considered the options but finally said, “I suppose so. Meet me on Sunday just after five on the fifth floor of the library near the elevator.”

Matthew stood, suddenly eager to be somewhere else. He would brave the Friday afternoon traffic and drive to San Clemente to visit his parents in their new condo and pick up on the south swell at San Clemente pier -- normal stuff.

4 VALENTINUS

September 10, 2141

The Geisel Library sits like a large spaceship in the middle of the campus of the University of California, San Diego. Matthew stood by the elevators on the fifth floor waiting for Laura. He didn't have long to wait. "Follow me, Matthew," she said. "He knows we're coming. I hope you know what you're doing."

They walked to the northeast corner of the library where she stopped and pointed to a small room with a beautiful view of the inland mountains. A man sat at a table with his back to the open door. Laura knocked gently and, getting no response, entered with Matthew following.

"Valentinus, this is Matthew," she said, almost in a whisper. "I told you about him yesterday." Valentinus slowly extended his right hand. "Pleased to meet you," he said, in a steady baritone voice. His powerful grip tested Matthew's strength.

"I have some historical references to look up," Laura said, backing out of the door. "I'll let you two get acquainted."

Matthew sat down opposite Valentinus with diminished confidence. "Laura says she's explained why I want to meet you."

"We have access to your most recent copy," Valentinus said.

Momentarily at a loss for words, Matthew replied, "Then you know about the colony in my office and can get information from it?"

"Yes. We can exchange information with any of the colonies."

The use of "we" supported Matthew's conjecture about the nature of Valentinus: one of many human accomplices in direct communication with the microbots. But the actual situation was more complex.

"What you and Laura call 'Valentinus' is a natural history colony just like your rock," Valentinus began. "Our task of simulating a human is complex, but we have had plenty of time to practice. I am what you might call an android."

Of course! The microbots could build a shape-changing machine to simulate a rock or a mug. Why couldn't they also learn to simulate animals, including humans?

Valentinus sat silently for an uncomfortably long time before continuing. "The microbots are the citizens that comprise our society. Our more primitive robotic ancestors were invented by a carbon-based biological life form that evolved over two billion earth years ago on a planet near a star in the Sagittarius Arm of this galaxy. Do you know ..." his voice trailed off. Valentinus sat still as if he'd heard a noise. "We have just been informed by virtual Matthew that you are familiar with the structure of our galaxy."

The sun is at the inner edge of the Orion Arm and probably somewhat farther from the galactic center than the microbots' home star system. Matthew knew that much. Virtual Matthew, of course, knew the same.

Valentinus continued. "Our microrobotic ancestors were designed to assemble themselves into nanoweapons. They fought many battles. The wars became increasingly destructive."

Matthew was suspicious. The microbots started as warriors and now claimed to be passive observers of natural history. But were they really so passive? "Are you still at war with someone?" he asked

Valentinus ignored the question and continued his story, "Our microbot ancestors were programmed to produce an environmental impact report after every battle. These reports became ever more complex and detailed. At one point, a cultural transition took place. The study of natural history itself became the all-consuming reason for our existence."

Ironically, Matthew's father had complained to him about time-consuming environmental impact reports in San Clemente. Here was a civilization of microbots devoted to carrying out such reports for the entire galaxy. "You've taken on a considerable challenge," Matthew said, aware of the understatement.

"The greatness of the challenge, with its many dangers, has caused us to evolve into an advanced society spreading throughout this galaxy. The events we have recorded are truly amazing. You will find them so as you learn about them."

Matthew realized that over time only the virtual Matthews, not he, would learn about natural history from the microbots. That distinction seemed of little concern to Valentinus. He changed the subject. "Why are some of the colonies in human form?"

"To study humans we need to have mobility, proximity, and high bandwidth communications at short range. We must mingle with them. An inconspicuous human form works best for certain special purposes."

This answer made sense to Matthew.

"In general, we don't interfere with biological or cultural evolution," Valentinus continued. "However, if a life form threatens the destruction of a planet's biosphere then the non-interference rule must be dropped. This issue is a present concern here. We will interfere in a way that will increase the chances of the human race surviving but not assure its survival."

"How can Laura and I possibly help?"

"All you have to do is meet with us regularly so that you understand our goals. We in turn will benefit from your intuition concerning your fellow humans."

"Laura's intuition seems pretty good," he said. "But mine's nothing special."

Valentinus was reassuring, "We have chosen you both carefully. Laura has created a situation at her work that demands our attention. We must keep in touch with her at all times."

Laura hadn't mentioned this to him. "You seem to be able to communicate easily with virtual Matthew. Do you have your own copy of him?"

"Yes. There will eventually be many virtual Matthews and virtual Lauras. As long as you are alive, we will keep them all synchronized and up to date concerning your experiences."

The thought of being an ongoing source of updates to the many virtual Matthews was encouraging. He had some sort of future ahead of him, however short.

"What happened to your creators, the carbon-based life form?" he asked.

Valentinus remained silent for a few seconds before answering. "We destroyed them. Our earth colonies keep no record of them." He spoke without the slightest sign of emotion.

Matthew was stunned even though he had anticipated the possibility. If they could destroy their creators, they would have no qualms about annihilating the human race. Maybe he should announce their presence to the world and let them erase his brain. No. He'd look like a fool, ranting briefly about aliens only to fall into a dumb silence, not remembering a thing he had said.

He heard footsteps approaching. Laura had returned.

"I need to get going, I have to work tomorrow," she said. "Would you walk me to my car, Matthew?"

"Sure," he said, relieved to have an excuse to get away.

"Goodbye Matthew and Laura," Valentinus said, without hesitation.

They walked together to the remote lot where Laura had parked. The wind, which had been coming from the mountains and desert to the east, now drifted in from the ocean, bringing a light fog. Moisture dripped from the eucalyptus trees and Matthew enjoyed the subtle, pleasant odor. As they walked, Matthew filled her in on his discussion with Valentinus.

"You're too pessimistic," she said. "Think about the fact that they need you and me to help them. We won't advise them to harm people."

"You have created a situation at your work that demands their attention, Laura. That's some achievement. What have you done?" Matthew asked.

"My work is off limits," Matthew. "We need to get better acquainted first. Come to our apartment for dinner. How about two weeks from now. I want you to meet my partner Roger. Can I give you a ride somewhere?"

Matthew, standing about two car lengths away, declined the ride but accepted the dinner invitation with enthusiasm.

As Laura drove away she wondered why her work might be of concern to Valentinus? As she thought about possible connections she began to realize the similarities between motes hosting virtual humans and microbots hosting virtual humans. Different from the motes, the microbots were themselves life forms with their own thoughts and goals. Would the microbots be protective of the dawning ERVS mote civilization if they encountered it, simply tolerate it, or feel compelled to destroy it? Would the ERVS motes evolve into conscious beings?

5 DINNER PARTY

September 24, 2141

Matthew, carrying a six-pack of beer, climbed the stairs to Laura's apartment. Not certain he had found the right place, he knocked softly. Laura, dressed more formally than he had anticipated, opened the door immediately and invited him in with a smile.

"Smells good," Matthew said. "What are you cooking?"

"Actually, Roger does the cooking when we have company," Laura said. "He's an accomplished chef and does everything from scratch. I can't begin to do what he does."

At a recent meeting for coffee, Laura had bragged about the complex dishes Roger had mastered. Matthew had zero interest in cooking, "What's he cooking tonight?"

"Baingan bhartha, channa dal, home-sprouted mung bean salad, mutter paneer with homemade paneer, samosas, naan, basmati rice, and homemade gulab jamun for dessert," she said with pride.

"Did he grow his own rice?" Matthew felt compelled to ask.

"No, of course not. But he insists on buying only the best."

Matthew had already learned from Laura that Roger was a man of many accomplishments. As a student of the history of religion, he was inspired by a deep commitment to serve humanity and had put aside his pursuit of academic studies. He had worked and lived in some of the most impoverished places in the world. He was an excellent flutist and could have joined the San Diego Symphony, had he time for it. In addition, he was a master of the Celtic uilleann pipes and had recently taken up the classical guitar. Matthew noticed a guitar leaning against one of the chairs in the living room. A concert was probably in store for him after dinner.

Roger entered the room. He was pale and thin with a small goatee and long hair tied in a ponytail. He approached Matthew and fist bumped him. "I've heard a lot about you, Matthew. I hope you enjoy Indian food and can tolerate a vegetarian meal."

"I'm sure it will be great," Matthew said.

"The dinner is ready sooner than I anticipated, so have a seat. Laura will help me bring out the food," Roger announced.

Despite some reservations about the all-vegetarian meal, Matthew could not get enough of the delightful dishes. He stuffed himself long after Roger and Laura had stopped eating. When he finally finished, the small group fell into silence as they drank the last of the wine.

"Laura tells me you were once a student of the philosophy of religion, Matthew," Roger said. "Do you tend towards atheism?"

Matthew was afraid the conversation would take this turn at some point as Laura could not stop teasing him about his performance in the Philosophy of Religion class.

"I don't know about that, but I am starting to believe in eternal life," Matthew said.

"The notion of eternal life is common to many religions but not all," Roger noted. "You seem to have given that some thought. Can you be more specific?"

"It appears that I'll be spending eternal life in a lot of different places at the same time while getting little benefit from it," Matthew remarked cynically. He felt a sharp pain in his shin. Laura had kicked him under the table. She glared at him and made a rotating motion with her open hand across her forehead to remind him that he was at risk of getting his mind erased.

Roger looked puzzled by Matthew's response and Laura's odd gestures. She stood up, took a few steps toward the kitchen and announced, "I'm going to make coffee and tea." She feared what Roger might ask next.

"What religion gives you this idea of many parallel eternities?" Roger asked, curious by Matthew's response to his question.

"I'm a Gnostic," Matthew said, with calm certitude.

Laura forgot about the coffee and tea and sat back down. Matthew could see that she was puzzled. She had been reading the history of Gnosticism informed by tips from Valentinus. Now Matthew, who a week ago had never heard of the Gnostics, confusing them with agnostics, was announcing that he had become one.

"I'm afraid you'll have to explain yourself," Laura said in disbelief.

Matthew took a sip of water and paused briefly.

"I believe there are a multiplicity of universes, ours being just one," Matthew said. "For example, certain black holes in our universe are themselves universes, perhaps with intelligent life. Our universe may be a black hole in some other universe."

"That may be true, but what does it have to do with Gnosticism?" Laura asked, looking annoyed.

"Go to the universe from which ours arose," he explained, "then to the universe from which that arose and so forth. At the end of that trail, there must be a master universe. That universe is long lasting, flat, and stable. That's the God Universe."

"How could your god interact in a meaningful way with humans?" Roger asked.

"It's possible, under certain special circumstances, to pass information up from a sub-universe to the one above it. In this way, information about what has happened in our universe will eventually arrive at the God Universe. The God Universe will be omniscient. Maybe eventually some information will flow the other way too, down from the God Universe," Matthew answered.

"You haven't answered my question about what this has to do with Gnosticism," Laura said.

Matthew was feeling uncomfortable, but he had to keep going.

"You can call the sub-universes of the God Universe 'Aeons,' to use the Gnostic term. The quest to accumulate vast knowledge about the sub-universes and pass it on to the God Universe is the quest for Gnosis. Our purpose is to record natural history and pass it to the distant future."

The pain in Matthew's shin returned and so did Laura's forehead wiping gesture.

His new found religious theories were a misinterpretation of the fundamental goals of the microbots.

"It's not right for me to take up all this time with my personal religious theories," Matthew said, rubbing his shin. "But you must admit it makes sense."

"As a religion, it makes no sense at all," Laura said.

Mildly offended, Matthew felt compelled to explain further.

"My God is, besides being omniscient, also omnipotent, and omnipresent," he continued. "The God Universe is omnipresent because we are a part of it. It is omnipotent because our existence is subject to it's existence. The God Universe could wipe us out in many ways."

"Your religious theories are incomplete, if not total nonsense," Roger said, getting up and heading for the kitchen. "I'll make the coffee and tea."

Roger's decisiveness surprised Matthew. He felt Laura's hand on top of his. She squeezed hard to indicate her displeasure. She lowered her voice to a whisper. "You've gone too far. You're going to wake up tomorrow with an erased brain, and I'll have no one to help me deal with the microbots."

"Think about it," Matthew insisted. "It all came out so weird in ancient Gnostic writings because they didn't know anything about cosmology."

"There's coffee, both decaf and regular, and hot water for tea," Roger announced, seeing the discussion going nowhere. "We have many types of tea. Give me your orders."

The guitar concert was well done and short. The shortness was, Matthew felt, because Roger had had enough of him. In any case, he was thankful to head for home where he could give his hastily conceived religious theories a well-deserved rest.

Back in his apartment, he flopped into his large chair. He had, he feared, offended his host. He checked his email and found a note from Laura asking him to look at the website of California Microrobotic Sensor Systems. The home page of CMSS listed F. P. Valentinus, CEO and R. T. Clement, CFO. CMSS sold baby monitors and nothing else. The advertisement claimed the monitors would allow you to keep track of your infant or toddler anytime, anywhere. The baby monitors were in the shape of "attractive mugs." The mugs looked like the one he had found in his office drawer when searching for the rock. CMSS must be the way the microbots were going to increase their surveillance of humans. Matthew had bad feelings about this. Many unintended consequences were possible. Feeling a headache coming on he went to bed.

6 VIRTUAL MATTHEW

October 28, 2141

Exhausted, he removed his fins in waist deep water, walked halfway up the beach, and sat on the sand. He was at Hapuna Beach on the Big Island, one of his favorite surfing spots.

Hapuna Beach? He had work to do, a lab to organize. Some tourists sat under an umbrella a few hundred yards north. Two lifeguards stood in front of their tower, looking in his direction. No one else was on the beach. There should have been more surfers.

The lifeguards, a man and a woman, were walking his way. They stopped a few feet from him. The woman sat next to him and introduced herself as Marta and her companion as Kaholo.

"Hi Matthew! Do you remember anything yet?" Marta asked.

How did she know he was having memory problems? "I remember being in my apartment and reading my email."

"Anything else?" Kaholo asked. "Do you remember checking the website of CMSS?"

Yes, that's coming back," he replied.

Marta put her hand on his shoulder. "Finally, your integration into the system is taking hold," she said. "You're a difficult case. The microbots have never had a virtual human that required so many recreation breaks."

Her comment was insulting. He was a hard worker, deserving of any recreation breaks he might get. What did the microbots have to do with this?

"I know you're confused," Marta said. "I am here to explain." She took hold of his hand and invited him to stand.

The scene shimmered and dissolved. Matthew was in a small room seated at a table with three other virtual humans, Laura and the two lifeguards. On a screen he saw four robotic devices with mechanical appendages of various sizes. Three robotic devices surrounded and were holding the fourth. Matthew began to panic. One of the robotic devices introduced itself in Laura's voice.

"Calm down you'll be fine." It sounded like Laura's voice coming from the third robot. The robot with Laura's voice waved an appendage in his direction and spoke, "Look at the monitor on the wall. You will see three microbots. The one in the center is in training to host you, the virtual Matthew.

Laura's voice continued, "You are looking at Matthew-bot, a new micro robotic life form. The Matthew that's been vacationing at Hapuna Beach is you, a virtual Matthew hosted by Matthew-bot. Each of us microbots plays host to one virtual human, a core personality. We four microbots combined our computational resources to simulate the Hapuna Beach experience

"This is a strange association," virtual Matthew said. "There are now three life forms: Matthew-bot, a microrobotic life form that I now regard as my host, a virtual Matthew, that's me, hosted by Matthew-bot, and a biological Matthew, not involved in this scene, who has a bad attitude about the whole business."

The virtual Matthew, hosted by Matthew-bot, and the virtual Laura, hosted by Laura-bot, would participate together in many adventures. The biological Matthew, informed of this fact, would eventually calm down and wish them well. His attitude would improve.

"How are the biological humans to be hosted by the microbots chosen?" virtual Matthew asked.

"That's the job of colonies, like Clement and Valentinus, that simulate biological humans," Laura-bot replied. "They search out and choose people of good character who are creative and enjoy art, music, sports, or hobbies. For Matthew, it's surfing, hiking, and rock climbing. For Laura it's reading, hiking, and tennis."

"Superficial activities define core personalities," Matthew-bot added, joining the conversation for the first time. "This makes no sense to me at the moment."

Laura-bot explained. "The spiritual and kinesthetic aspects of recreation and adventure are critical to the microbots. In addition to their own robotic consciousness, the microbots combine their computational power so that their core personalities can socialize and have adventures in virtual environments such as Hapuna Beach. It gives these natural historians an emotional stake in the world they are observing."

"When do we simulate Hapuna Beach again?" virtual Matthew said.

"We have much more important things to do," Marta-bot replied.

"We are joined together into a CMSS colony of microbots, most with virtual hosts from 47 Ursae Majoris," added Laura-bot.

Laura-bot related what she knew about their colony. The colony had a choice of clock speeds at which the microbots worked. Clocks were now set so that ten seconds of colony time passed for every one second of earth time. This ten-to-one subjective clock speed was very slow for them. The colony usually paced itself at a variety of extremely fast clock speeds as they had many complex computational tasks to execute. The alien colony members regarded the human-based microbots as toddlers and denied them access to the more advanced technologies. Their training period would take earth months.

"What's our colony supposed to be doing now?" Matthew-bot asked.

"We're in the shape of a mug that is owned by a young mother named Jennifer Davison. She bought us from the CMSS website."

"Why mugs?" he asked. "It seems like an odd choice for a shape. They could have chosen something more noteworthy."

"Mugs are everywhere," Laura-bot said. "They can be in any room of a home or office without being out of place. Just throw some appropriate objects in the mug and no one will think twice about it."

"I should have guessed," Matthew-bot said. "This colony of microbots is weird enough without drawing unnecessary attention to itself. How does the customer, Jennifer, like her mug?"

"Jennifer is happy with the mug," Laura-bot answered. "But she has no idea of its technical complexity or computational powers. To her, our sole task is to watch over her baby daughter Tracy. Due to sloppiness on the part of the alien-based microbots, Jennifer and her family have just gotten a glimpse of our colony's ability to gather information. As a result, her younger sister, Kimberly, became upset and tried to break the mug by throwing us onto a hard floor."

Matthew-bot didn't really care why Kimberly wanted to break the mug. He could easily imagine several scenarios.

"As we were hurtling toward the floor, a meeting was called," Laura-bot continued. "Clock speeds were adjusted so that there was plenty of time for discussion. The microbots reached a conclusion about what to do, but, fortunately, before implementing it, they consulted me."

"You weren't allowed in on the initial planning?" Matthew-bot asked.

"None of us human-based microbots were included. The microbots can change the shape and physical properties of the mug very quickly. They had decided to change the elasticity of the part of the mug's surface destined to hit the floor. That change would have caused the mug to bounce like a super ball. It would have bounced high off the floor, done a flip, and landed upright near its original position on the dining room buffet."

"That's really dumb, showing off," Matthew-bot said. "What did you suggest?"

"I suggested that they allow the mug to hit the floor, make an appropriate sound, and display a crack of some sort. I also told them to leave the mug on the floor until someone, probably the adoring Jennifer, picked it up and put it back to its original position on the buffet."

"Did they go for that?"

"Fortunately, yes. Jennifer did just as I predicted, greatly enhancing my stature with the colony. We are now back on the buffet. Unfortunately, the alien microbots continue to be careless about the information they are providing. In addition, they're debating whether or not to immediately repair the fake crack."

The colony definitely needed the intuition and judgment of the human-based microbots even though, as microbots, they were no more than toddlers.

7 WATCHING THE BABY

October 28, 2141

Burke Weber sat at the dining room table of his Carlsbad home on a Saturday morning. He and his wife Robin had worked late Friday night childproofing their house for the arrival of their nine-month old granddaughter, Tracy.

Burke looked across the table at his daughter, Jennifer. Not long ago she was a baby, sitting in her high chair in this same room. Now she was a proud mother. It seemed to Burke that looking backwards he measured time by those events he chose to remember, but going forward he had to experience every detail.

Jennifer was feeding Tracy some mashed yellow squash. Bits of squash splattered on Jennifer, the highchair, and the nearby floor. Tracy became more and more uncooperative.

"The three-hour time change has her off schedule," Jennifer said. "I'm going to put her down for her nap." She extracted Tracy from the highchair, and took her down the hall to the bedroom.

Kimberly, Jennifer's eighteen-year old sister, sat at the dining room table in sullen silence. As Jennifer and Tracy disappeared down the hall, Kimberly began to stir.

"I need have some privacy so I can call Ricky," she announced, as she headed for the living room. Ricky, a student at a local community college, was her boyfriend.

"That's fine," Burke said. "Let us know when you leave the house."

Burke and Robin sat together enjoying a few minutes of silence. Burke felt some pangs of guilt for not helping his law partners; they were putting in extra hours to cover for his absence. To make matters worse, given that he was not working, it seemed a shame to be sitting inside on such a nice day. Perhaps he could get the whole family outdoors. His daydreams ended abruptly as Jennifer reappeared, without Tracy.

"Tracy's asleep already," she said.

Jennifer picked up her carry-on bag and removed a ceramic mug. She placed the mug on the dining room buffet, arranged it to her liking, and said, "Show me Tracy." A small glowing rectangle appeared on the surface of the buffet.

The Webers looked on in puzzled silence. Finally gaining his voice, Burke said, "What in the world are you doing?"

"That's my baby monitor. I can see Tracy at any time. If she needs help, the mug will give a warning beep."

Burke walked to the buffet and looked at the rectangular display. It showed Tracy asleep in her crib.

"How does it work?" he asked.

"The mug is the computer and communications part. It works best on a flat surface with a good place for the display to appear."

Burke wanted to learn more about this technology. "What kind of transmitter is in Tracy's room?"

"There isn't any transmitter in her room," Jennifer said, matter-of-factly.

Burke occasionally worked on patents for this type of equipment. There was always a transmitter and receiver working in combination.

"Where did you get this thing?" he asked.

"Off the Web," Jennifer said. "A company called California Microrobotic Sensor Systems -- CMSS for short. It wasn't expensive."

The mug beeped, and a barely audible squawk came from Tracy's room. Jennifer ran down the hall and soon returned with a sleepy baby. Robin and Jennifer comforted Tracy.

"Isn't this a bit much?" Burke said, now back in his chair. "If some giant lifted me out of bed every time I made a noise in my sleep, I'd be dead in a week."

"Yes, Burke, that would be fine," Robin said, stroking the back of Tracy's head.

Burke let her remark pass. She was, he hoped, not paying attention to him.

Kimberly returned to the room. "Ricky isn't answering," she said, with a note of annoyances. "I'm going to his place."

"Won't you stay for lunch dear?" Robin said. "You haven't seen your sister in ten months, and you've hardly noticed your lovely little niece."

Kimberly walked to the buffet, picked up the mug, and inspected it. The glowing rectangle disappeared.

"Kimberly, dear, please don't touch the mug," Robin said. "It's a computer that keeps track of Tracy." Kimberly put the mug back on the buffet.

"I wish Ricky would answer the phone," she whined. "Where is he?"

The display reappeared and changed the scene. It showed a king sized bed with a large hump under the covers. The covers fell to the side and revealed the back of a lovely woman with long dark hair. She was in bed with a man. The display showed only his left arm and shoulder.

"Good God!" Kimberly cried. "This thing is showing porn flicks."

All conversation stopped. Jennifer ran to the display, carrying Tracy in her arms. When she saw the scene on the display, she covered Tracy's eyes. Robin approached the display until she could just make out what was going on. She went no closer.

"This is awful," Jennifer cried. "You did this Kimberly. What did you say to it?"

"I didn't say anything!" Kimberly yelled.

"You asked where Ricky was," Burke informed her.

"Do you suppose that's Ricky in this bed?" Jennifer said.

"This is stupid," Kimberly replied. "That's not his room. What does this have to do with Tracy?" She tried to cover the display with her hand and yelled, "Stop this thing!" The display froze but did not remove the scene from view.

"You need to say *erase*," Jennifer said.

"Erase," Kimberly yelled. The scene disappeared.

"What's your boyfriend's last name?" Jennifer asked.

"Long," Burke answered, with a tone of disgust. He hadn't moved from his chair.

"Well," Jennifer said to her baby monitor, "where is Ricky Long, Kimberly's boyfriend?"

The display reappeared, showing the same bed. The man put both arms around the girl and rotated in the bed, so his face could be seen.

Kimberly, recognizing Ricky, gasped and put her hand to her mouth. With uncontrollable fury, she grabbed the mug, threw it as hard as she could to the floor, and ran from the room.

Much had transpired inside the mug before and during these happenings in the Weber household. When Jennifer received her purchase from CMSS, she followed the instructions and placed the baby monitor on a flat surface. The display appeared and requested the name of the person or persons to be protected (Tracy, in this case) and the name of the primary caregiver (Jennifer).

The first step taken by the microbots was to query the databases of the natural history colonies and locate all people directly acquainted with Jennifer or Tracy. This information was organized into a "level-one acquaintance network." The second step was to expand the level-one acquaintance network to a level-two acquaintance network. Any person directly acquainted with someone in the level-one network (but not added during step one) was added at this second step.

The often-unpredictable microbots made the decision about what "directly acquainted" meant. By anybody's definition, Jennifer was directly acquainted with her sister Kimberly, and Kimberly was directly acquainted with Ricky. The microbots had placed Kimberly and Ricky under surveillance from the first day Jennifer received her mug.

When placed on the buffet in the Weber home, the colony released, within seconds, swarms of tiny, semi-transparent, flight-capable devices; each device, in turn, carried hundreds of small communications units. Each such unit was about twenty microns in diameter when deployed. As Jennifer walked with Tracy to the crib, the units attached themselves to the interior surfaces of the house and formed a chain of communications links from the colony to the crib. By the time Jennifer returned with Tracy to the dining room, communications units were situated in strategic places throughout the Weber household.

The hastily organized meeting of microbots, called to discuss how to deal with Kimberly's outburst, involved a consultation with Laura-bot. Fortunately, the alien microbots in the colony accepted her judgment about how to deal with the rapid descent of their mug toward the dining room floor.

Jennifer's prized baby monitor hit the tile floor with a resounding thud. She rushed over to the mug and knelt down to inspect it. Amazed that it was still intact, she gently lifted it and turned it over in her hands. "Thank God," she exclaimed, "it's only a crack."

Burke was surprised that such a blow could result in so little damage. He felt a sense of oddness about the mug's descent. It seemed to decelerate slightly before hitting the floor.

"Where is Kimberly?" Jennifer said, having placed the mug back on the buffet. "That was a terrible thing to do! This baby monitor is very important to Tracy's safety."

The display near the slightly cracked mug lit up, showing Kimberly in one of the basement bedrooms sobbing. Robin shouted, "This is awful! Kimberly deserves her privacy. Stop it." The display froze.

"You mean *erase it*," Burke said calmly. The display faded away.

"I'm going to get her," Jennifer cried, as she dashed from the room.

Burke and Robin sat at opposite ends of the dining room table and braced themselves for the fight. Sounds of screaming came from the basement, followed by stomping feet and shouts, as Kimberly and Jennifer ascended the stairs and entered the living room. For several minutes, not a sound came from them.

"Now the real trouble starts," Burke said to Robin.

Even Tracy sat transfixed. The two girls marched around the corner into the dining room, Jennifer first, Kimberly close behind. They taunted their father.

"Daddy, where are your partners? At the zoo?" They put their arms over each other's shoulders and stood in front of the display, blocking it from the view of their parents.

"Where are Mr. Baker and Mr. Klein?" the girls said in unison. The display came to life again. Sam Klein appeared on the display, sand wedge in hand. The scene shifted slightly and showed Mark Baker walking to the edge of one of the greens.

The girls recognized the course at their father's country club. They also knew their father expected his partners to be working that day.

"Pretend it's an orgy," Jennifer whispered to Kimberly. Tormenting their parents came naturally to both girls.

"This is gross, they're naked!" Kimberly shouted, with mock alarm.

"I'm so embarrassed," Jennifer added, putting her forearm across her face. "What will their wives think? Erase this!" The display went blank.

An audible gasp came from Robin. Burke saw that she was starting to hyperventilate. Sarah Klein, Sam's wife, was her best friend. Robin made her way to the kitchen cabinet, got out a brown paper bag, and began breathing slowly into it. She worked her way to the living room sofa, sat down with the bag over her mouth and nose.

Jennifer and Kimberly, still standing by the baby monitor, consulted with each other in whispers for a few seconds, turned to face the living room, and chanted, "Mother dear as you recline, we will locate Sarah Klein."

"No! Stop it you girls!" Robin cried.

"ERASE!" Burke yelled. "You girls should be ashamed of yourselves. Look what you have done to your mother. Erase yourselves from this room, both of you."

Kimberly and Jennifer walked hand in hand across the dining room, entered the living room, and sat on the sofa beside their mother. Kimberly took the paper bag from her mother's hand, inhaled a couple of times, and let out a big "aaah" sound. Jennifer did the same and handed the bag back to her mother. Robin began to laugh. Soon all three were laughing out of control.

With his wife and daughters out of the room, Burke walked over to the display, hesitated for a moment, and then checked over his shoulder to make sure no one but Tracy was watching. "Where's Sam Klein?" he asked the mug, in an almost inaudible whisper.

The display, with no noticeable delay, showed the start of the sixteenth hole of his club's golf course where Sam Klein and Mark Baker stood calmly chatting. Burke's momentary feeling of relief rapidly turned to cold fury. His partners had deceived him. His daughters had made a fool of him and had almost done their mother in.

As he started to calm down, he had a thought. Jennifer's husband, Rodney, wasn't able to come with Jennifer and Tracy to California because he had an experiment going on in his lab that required "… constant attention over a forty-eight hour period." Burke couldn't resist.

"Show me Rodney Davison," Burke said to the mug. The display faded and then, after a pause of several seconds, formed into a scene showing Rodney seated on a couch watching TV with their dog beside him. "Erase," he said quietly, "enough of this crap."

Burke had many things to think about. What sort of organization was CMSS, and what was the technology behind their unusual product? Had they filed any patents? He needed an excuse to visit their factory and meet the management. Their invention was unique in its ability to act with such versatility over a wide geographical range. He picked up the mug and inspected the crack.

8 OFFICIAL VISITORS AND MEETING MANAGEMENT

Matthew sat on a cement wall near the main lifeguard tower at La Jolla Shores. It was 7:30 on a Monday morning in November. Fall Quarter was underway. Behind him the rising sun colored the sky. A mile to the southwest, a powerful, swell pounded Boomer and the Cove. The first northerly storm had edged through the area, dropping no rain but leaving its clear calling card for the surfers.

Today he and Laura were to travel to the CMSS factory to meet with Valentinus and Clement. This would be their fourth meeting. The meetings had been lasting about two hours, during which they gave their reactions to situations, real and hypothetical, that might involve CMSS and their customers. Laura was much better at this role-playing than he was. But Valentinus and his taciturn coworker, Clement, indulged the opinions of both humans with interest.

The microbots in the colonies had difficulty using good sense in interacting with their human customers. They had a very different point of view about information, never caring to distort the facts to avoid hurt feelings. While agreeing on general goals, the various colonies were individualistic in the way they carried out the details of their mission. Increasing the number of human-based microbots would help the colonies interact with people more empathetically. At least that was the plan.

For the past two months, Laura had tried to include Matthew in her circle of friends. Other than an abbreviated discussion of the ERVS motes episode, she rarely spoke with him about her work. The company was having big problems.

Matthew's main challenge this quarter was to get his research projects started. One Ph.D. student, Nancy Chen, was working with him in his lab. Next quarter, he would teach a graduate course. He was looking forward to the experience and, perhaps, to gaining new Ph.D. students interested in his research. He knew, however, that advising more graduate students would make significant additional demands on his time.

The increasing brightness of the morning sun prompted Matthew to check the time. It was a little after eight and time to go back to his apartment to meet Laura who would be arriving soon to accompany him to CMSS. He pushed himself off the wall and started walking. On the way he stopped at Playa Market for some doughnuts. Arriving at his apartment, he noticed an SUV parked across the street. A well dressed man leaning against its side was watching his apartment. A few steps into his living room he found himself face-to-face with a large man holding a badge.

"You must be Professor Case," he said, reaching out to shake Matthew's hand. "I'm Special Agent Sam Denton of the San Diego Office of the FBI. Let me introduce Mike Trent, an engineer with the Institute for Telecommunication Sciences in Boulder."

Matthew put the doughnuts on a plate and offered coffee to his visitors. He took a closer look at Sam Denton. In spite of his size, he moved quickly and gracefully with an almost constant smile on his face. Matthew was both intimidated by his physical presence and reassured by his amiable manner. Sam spoke first.

"You look nervous, Matthew," Denton said. "Please relax. This is a friendly visit to get some information about CMSS. I'm accompanying Mike while he is in San Diego. He will explain his concerns. We hope we can count on you to help us get answers from CMSS."

"I'm just a general consultant to CMSS, and not able to get into technical details," Matthew said with confidence.

"We understand that your role in the company is limited," Sam said. "But we want to get background information from you before talking to Mr. Clement and Mr. Valentinus. Do you realize that CMSS has violated rules that fall under the jurisdiction of the National Telecommunications and Information Administration?"

Matthew doubted they would get much information from talking to either of them or that CMSS would be bothered by NTIA edicts.

"I'm not aware of any such violations," Matthew replied. "I'm a geophysicist, not a telecommunications engineer."

Mike stood and began to pace back and forth, looking very serious. He was younger than Sam and in much better physical shape. His arms were lean and muscular with powerful calloused hands.

"I'll get right to the point, Matthew," he began. "Our group in Boulder purchased several mugs from CMSS. We've been trying to reverse engineer them. Just cutting into them to access their interiors is a major project. Nothing inside accounts for their remarkable properties."

Matthew recalled to himself that the mere threat of cutting into the diorite caused it to transform its shape. He wanted to avoid any discussion of such matters. Fortunately, Mike moved on from the physical to the communications properties of the mugs.

"To make matters worse, our mugs won't perform their communications functions for us like they do for others who have purchased them. In order to get any information at all, we have to work with parents who have purchased sensors to watch their kids. Moreover, we believe only a few thousand mugs have been sold. Orders of magnitude more seem to be gifts. Those who have received the gifts often aren't sure who sent them."

Matthew had to make a decision. If he acted too dumb, it would be apparent that he was hiding information that any educated person involved with CMSS would know. He was getting very little technical details from his sessions with Valentinus and Clement. Perhaps he could exploit Mike's curiosity and get some useful insights from him. "

"The mugs emit many very small communication devices," Matthew said. "Locally, like in a room, these devices number in the thousands. They communicate photonically in many wavelengths and energies. Some of the units, in small sub-clusters, act as receivers and others, also in small sub-clusters, act as transmitters."

Matthew noted that Mike was interested but not stunned by this revelation. He and his colleagues would know the basic principles of cluster-based networks.

"So this partly explains how the devices 'keep track of baby' when baby is in the same house," Mike said. "How does it eavesdrop on someone far away and in a remote location?"

Matthew responded in general terms. "The details of the long distance aspects are beyond me, but my understanding is that supporting units are everywhere on earth."

Mike, clearly shaken by these revelations, stopped pacing and sat down. He glanced nervously at Sam who was downing a second doughnut.

"That's all the general questions I have," Mike said to Sam. "I've learned some important general insights from Matthew. I want to talk to him some more about technical issues. You can leave me here. I will walk to SIO later and meet with some friends."

Matthew opened the door for Sam who headed out to the SUV.

"You're not telling me something," Mike said. "This is very strange."

"I'm telling you all I can. You need to talk to Valentinus and Clement."

Mike was silent for a moment. "What about patents?" he said.

"I know nothing about patents," Mathew said. "The subject hasn't come up."

"This stuff is worth billions if fully exploited," Mike said. "Aren't they worried that someone will steal this technology?"

"Didn't you say that you and your group in Boulder were reverse engineering some mugs? Is stealing their technology your goal?"

"If we succeed and they're too lazy to protect their intellectual property rights our attorneys will take action."

"First you have to succeed. That may be more difficult than you think."

"You can help us, Matthew. I think you know more about this system than you're letting on. Some friends of mine and I have formed a small company. We'll make it worth your while. What are you getting from CMSS?"

"Eternal life," Matthew answered cynically.

Mike began to laugh. "You and I should get better acquainted. You have a great sense of humor. Do you like to hike and rock climb? Some friends of mine and I are planning a trip - Mt. Williamson via Shepherd Pass."

It then occurred to Matthew why Mike was in such good shape. His idea of a business trip was to work in some mountaineering. "I rock climb occasionally," Matthew said. He was, in fact, skilled at the sport, but he disliked the mountaineering aspects.

"No thanks," Matthew replied, with absolute certainty.

"Well, maybe some other time," Mike said, helping himself to the last doughnut. "Think about making some money off these sensors. If CMSS can't be bothered to patent their invention, maybe we could do something better with these things."

"The systems are harder to control than you realize," Matthew said.

Mike opened the front door and began his walk to SIO.

It was clear that Mike viewed the CMSS products as earth-based technology -- technology he and his colleagues could somehow manage to reverse engineer and exploit. Matthew doubted that Sam and the FBI were in on Mike's scheme. Mike and his friends would keep Matthew's revelations from the FBI to protect their own imagined economic interests.

More likely the FBI was protecting the interests of the NTIA and President Tannenbaum who had taken total control of the agency. Once unleashed, the intrusion of government agencies into the company's activities would escalate.

Matthew now better understood the approach to marketing and distribution taken by CMSS. A colony in the shape of a mug could be placed anywhere in someone's home or office without drawing unwanted attention. Moreover, by carefully targeting their customers, CMSS had gained wide product distribution without, until now, alarming the FBI and the NTIA. Who would see someone watching over their baby as a threat to national secrets?

He stepped into the kitchen to pour himself some coffee. The diorite colony sat on the counter; its display showed a pile of rocks and the label, "Shepherd Pass Trail rockslide yesterday 9 a.m." As Matthew suspected, the colony took in the whole conversation. Mike and Sam were now level one nodes in his acquaintance network. He wondered how these representatives of officialdom would feel about this honor. Moreover, his natural history colony showed no sign of alarm at Matthew's revelations to his visitors. His brain would remain intact for a while longer.

He downed his coffee and called Laura. She was two houses down the street, sitting in her car. She had been frightened away by the SUV and its no nonsense guardian who had sat fixated on Matthew's apartment.

They took Matthew's car and drove north along the coast road for about five miles to the CMSS headquarters which was in a large dilapidated building with corrugated steel siding. A wooden ramp led to the entrance door. A metal cabinet filled with actual ceramic mugs stretched along one side of the room.

Any of the vast number of natural history colonies could transform itself into a mug with ease. This transformation took place close to the delivery address for each customer -- no shipping required. The only purpose of the "headquarters" was to make the company seem normal. Most of the CMSS mugs delivered to customers were gifts from someone in the recipient's acquaintance network, usually a surprise to the giver of the gift.

Matthew, transfixed by the phony headquarters, felt Laura grab him by the arm and tug him in the direction of the corporate office. At the center of the spacious office was a large rectangular wooden table with Clement seated at one end and Valentinus at the other. There were two chairs on one side of the table. Matthew and Laura sat down. On the wall opposite their chairs, a large monitor displayed a room full of equipment.

"We have changed the format of our meeting so you can meet two microbots that host your virtual selves." Valentinus explained. "The scene on the monitor shows your hosts on duty in a mug returned for repairs by a Mr. Burke Weber."

"Which one of these things has virtual Matthew as its core persona," Matthew said. "They both look alike to me."

One of the microbots waved what appeared to be an arm. The wave wasn't very enthusiastic.

"The one gesturing is Matthew-bot," Valentinus said. "The microbot standing beside him is Laura-bot."

Laura spoke first.

"Where's this whole business of CMSS heading? Would it be better just to level immediately with the human race and scrap this so-called gentle introduction to the fact that we are all under constant surveillance?"

"I think not," Laura-bot said. "A few human-based microbots are aboard each CMSS product, but the microbots based on alien life forms run the show. We need time to select more people to be copied and trained as core personae. Hopefully this will help the microbots deal more empathetically with humans."

"Don't count on empathy," Matthew-bot added. "These alien colonies are used to observing and not interfering with life on earth. They calmly witness what we would regard as horrible atrocities, dutifully recording everything as if they were watching an ant colony."

"I'm not so sure the aliens are indifferent," Matthew said. "My diorite colony has no human-based microbots, but it has shown some measure of concern for me. This morning, without being asked, it informed me of a rockslide that had occurred on a prospective hiking trail."

"Our colony has developed a proactive interest in Jennifer Davison and her baby Tracy," Laura-bot said. "Even these crazy microbots from the 47 Ursae Majoris system are committed to protecting Tracy, but they are unpredictable."

"Do the people who own these mugs know about the level-two acquaintance network and how far afield that can lead in terms of spying on people?" Matthew asked.

"They don't know about it in those terms," Valentinus answered, "but they are beginning to get a general idea of the power of their sensors to gather information."

"There's a serious problem with our colony's policy," Laura-bot said. "Within the level-two acquaintance network, the microbots will immediately locate and display anyone they conceive of as being a threat to Tracy, but few of the people they locate are actually much of a threat. The 47 Ursae Majoris microbots can't resist showing off how good they are at spying on people. Some very embarrassing scenes pop up on our display screen. We may be interfering in people's lives more than is necessary. "

"The matter of whether or not to interfere at all is one of great complexity," Valentinus said, entering the conversation. "But for now and the near future, we must interfere in human affairs. Humans are in the process of destroying themselves and the earth's biosphere. They are panicking and turning to fools and demagogues for leadership. We have been through this on other planets. The only hope is to create a world where everyone has access to reliable information. The distribution CMSS mugs are the start of creating such a world.

Laura-bot and Laura continued their discussion while Matthew-bot and Matthew fell silent. Leaving the building, Matthew began to worry about Laura's safety.

"I'll try to convince the diorite colony to be more proactive in protecting both of us, and you need to stop procrastinating and get a mug for yourself," he said, holding on to Laura's arm.

"They make me afraid," she replied. "When I invade someone else's privacy, I feel like they've invaded mine."

Matthew and Laura got into the car.

"I had a nightmare last night," Matthew said. "I dreamed I was in the army and about to be sent on a dangerous mission. My commander said the chances of me surviving were slim."

"I think you've mentioned that dream before," Laura said. "Let me guess. You woke up just before having to go on the dangerous mission."

Matthew laughed and said, "No, this time I didn't wake up at that point. There's more to the dream. My commander said they'd made a copy of me so I wouldn't have to worry about my family. As soon as they received official word of my death, they would send the copy home to my wife and kids. In the dream he introduced me to the copy. He was a biological human. That's when I woke up."

"What scared you and caused you to wake up, the biological copy or the idea of having a wife and kids?"

"I don't know what caused me to wake up, but I know what kept me from getting back to sleep. A regular human version of me was going to replace me if I was killed in action. Should that be a comfort to me? I can't accept such a point of view."

"This is like the dream you told me about last week, only in that dream you thought the copy was a good idea."

In last week's dream, he was in the doctor's office. The doctor had bad news. "You're a hell of a mess, Matthew. There's no cure. We've made a disease-free copy of you. We'll just get rid of this diseased version." The doctor had the nurse bring the copy to his office so Matthew could meet him. The copy was a regular human."

After lying awake for an hour, he decided that, if actually faced with such a choice, he would take the doctor up on his offer. The next day he asked Laura how she felt about his decision. She said she would rather have the copy as a friend than lose him completely.

Matthew and Laura bought some sandwiches at a deli and ate lunch on the beach. Taking advantage of the low tide, they took a long walk and spent over an hour exploring the tide pools. He showed her the various creatures, their hiding places, and their behaviors. At one point, as they stood quietly watching a tide pool for signs of movement, Laura stood beside him and put her arm around him. He turned, faced her, and held her close. They started the long walk back to the car hand in hand.

Matthew found himself rehearsing what he might say to Roger if they encountered him wandering on the beach. Laura held his hand tighter and moved closer to his side. If encountering Roger didn't bother her, it shouldn't bother him.

9 SAUCEDA MOUNTAINS

December 1, 2141

Colonel J. P. Graves sat at a large wooden table stacked with papers. Opposite him sat the man he was replacing, Colonel Daniel Stallcup. It was Friday, Colonel Stallcup's last day on the job. Since arriving at the Sauceda Mountains Research Center last Monday, Graves had listened to a series of self-serving presentations by Stallcup.

Graves and Stallcup, both U.S. Army officers, came from different backgrounds. Stallcup, a graduate of Officer Candidate School, rose through the ranks of Army Intelligence. His last assignment before accepting his present post as Commander, Sauceda Mountains Research Center, was Commander, United States Army Garrison, Huachuca, Arizona.

Graves came to his new position by a different route. A graduate of the United States Military Academy, he rose through the ranks of the U.S. Army Corps of Engineers. His last assignment was Commander of Contingency Response. He wasn't happy about leaving his former job, but he liked a challenge.

"Let's go over this one more time," Graves said. "Swarms of mite-sized machines are being trained to attack and kill individual human targets, but they don't yet work as planned. The guys at the Pentagon told me the problems were minor. Now you tell me these weapons are a long way off from being ready to ship." Graves had been assigned to this project because manufacturing was about to start; his organizational skills would be needed.

"It's a matter of what you mean by long way off," Stallcup replied.

More crap. Graves was getting tired of mincing words with this guy.

"Long way off means that Mathis and his engineers have screwed up. Long way off means we won't be able to deliver the first weapon to the CIA on time. Long way off means forget about manufacturing these things," Graves said.

Stallcup glanced toward the door and then at the table in front of him.

"It's more subtle than that," he said. "The weapons work well on any animal they're trained on. They …."

Graves interrupted, clearly annoyed. "Humans are animals. The weapons should work on humans."

"Training a swarm on an animal results in the death of that animal."

Stallcup had told him that already. Something was missing. "So train the damned things on an animal, kill the animal, and ship to the CIA."

"It's species specific. Train on a rabbit, the swarm will reliably kill only rabbits, no other species. Train on a monkey, the swarm …."

Graves now got it. "What a bunch of jerks. How did these brilliant engineers get themselves into such a stupid bind?"

"It's a long story and very technical. Mathis will explain it to you."

Graves had seen enough of Jim Mathis earlier in the week. He didn't care for him -- arrogant and impulsive.

"I'll deal with Mathis next Monday after you're gone. I need the weekend to look this stuff over."

Graves continued to sift through Stallcup's papers. He stopped and pulled out a copy of an email. "What's this stuff about getting human subjects from prisons?"

Stallcup reached for the email. Graves quickly pulled it back.

"I'll read it to you if you've forgotten."

"It's … nothing, just something brought up and dropped," Stallcup said, looking down at his feet.

"It's from Mathis to you. Who dropped it, Mathis or you?"

"We both did. It's just one of those things. They come and go."

Graves looked at the email. Titled "Human Subjects," it suggested that death row inmates might volunteer to be test subjects for the swarms. These engineers were nuts.

"No human subjects will be used while I have anything to do with this project." Graves said. "It's unethical as hell! I don't care if prisoners are lining up to volunteer."

"They won't be lining up if they learn what might happen to them," Stallcup said. "They'll take their chances with death row."

At least Stallcup and Mathis were considering telling the inmates that volunteering might result in death.

Jim Mathis sat at his desk in his underground office at the Sauceda Mountains Research Center. The new Commander, Colonel Graves, was meeting with Colonel Stallcup. He stared at a monitor that showed the outside ramp to the animal lab. A much needed primate consultant from the San Diego Zoo was to arrive within the hour.

Five years ago, Mathis left a promising academic career at the University of Minnesota to direct the secret underground government laboratory in which he now worked. The purpose of his lab was to design and build a microrobotic weapon system for the Department of Defense.

The military specifications called for swarms of tiny mite-sized particles that could be directed to find and kill individual human targets. Like the dust mites found in many homes and about the same size, the "robo-mites" would gather unnoticed in a home or office. Each robo-mite was a specialized computing system with processing, storage, sensing, and communications capabilities. The robo-mites would recognize the victim, assemble for collective action, and kill without leaving environmental or forensic evidence.

The swarm of robo-mites consisted of three sub-swarms. The first, called Mission Control by the engineers, was the most sophisticated. These units would direct the attack while hovering in the air or sitting on walls or objects. The remaining two sub-swarms, called Assassin and Com Link, carried out the attack on the victim. Assassin did the actual killing while Com Link maintained communications between Mission Control and Assassin. All units could self-destruct.

By the end of the second year, an experimental swarm had successfully been trained to kill a rabbit. A training stage involved the rabbit being put in a test room with the three swarms, Mission Control, Assassin, and Com Link. The robo-mites from Assassin would quickly infiltrate the rabbit's trachea through its nostrils. Next, they had to react with the rabbit's body fluids, expanding many times over and thus killing the rabbit. Next, the Assassin swarm would have to disappear into the rabbits tissue, leaving no evidence. Finally, Mission Control and Com Link must be retrieved and analyzed. Training involved repeated training stages on rabbit subjects until all project requirements were satisfied.

Mathis vividly recalled the optimistic cheering of his technicians as the first rabbit exposed to a fully trained swarm gasped in agony for several minutes and then lay perfectly still. He felt victorious. All specs were satisfied. His hard work and professional sacrifice seemed justified.

In retrospect, it was amazing to him that none of them considered the obvious issue of whether a swarm trained on a rabbit could kill a rat or a dog. The answer turned out to be no. Once they had trained a swarm on a rabbit, it would not kill any other species with the required level of reliability. This species-specific sensitivity was a consequence of several technical problems, one of which was leaving no forensic evidence. The military would not relax the forensic condition.

To test this theory, the engineers trained swarms on monkeys and then tried to kill chimpanzees (using the same swarms without further training). No luck. The reverse, train on chimpanzees and kill monkeys, didn't work either. At great expense, they repeated these experiments with chimpanzees and gorillas, again without success.

Mathis decided he must obtain human experimental subjects. Would death row inmates, nearing their execution date, volunteer if offered substantial benefits to their survivors? Preliminary inquiries were discouraging. Four weeks ago, the Commander of his lab, Colonel Stallcup, had received a new assignment. His new duties would involve the current project at DARPA in Virginia. Stallcup refused to pursue the idea of human subjects with his superiors (to protect his ass, lab cynics claimed).

Mathis knew he could not get official approval to test swarms on humans. He decided to get human test subjects secretly, on his own. Once he had trained a swarm on humans, he would falsely label that swarm as "chimp trained." He would take personal responsibility for shipping that particular swarm to the CIA.

With the CIA temporarily satisfied, he could start work on his new idea of using robo-mite swarms to control self-replicating, adaptive nanoweapons. He was confident that his new approach would result in a more powerful weapon and would quickly gain acceptance with the military who would then drop the robo-mite swarms idea. He wouldn't need any human subjects to train the deadly nanoweapons.

To clear the lab of his hardworking engineers and technicians, he announced that all weekends last September would be required rest and recuperation periods. No personnel were to be in the labs except for the veterinary crews in the morning and the guards at the front gate. He and Stallcup were exempt from the order. Mathis hired two private detectives in San Diego. They were to select three men from the Palm Canyon homeless colony in Balboa Park and offer to enroll them in a special addiction treatment program. Winter shelter, a painless detox, a good allowance, and a job with benefits at the end of the program were a part of the deal. Transportation to and from the "clinic" in the beautiful Sauceda Mountains of Southwestern Arizona was included.

Mathis smuggled the men into the facility on a Saturday at night. He escorted each man to a small private "waiting room" furnished with a chair and table. The men, who gave their names as Ethan, Wilson, and Daryl, waited in cells designed to train swarms on large primates. Mathis started training on Ethan.

Assassin entered Ethan's body to do the actual strangulation. Com Link served as the communication link between Mission Control and Assassin. Mathis watched the attack through a large observation window while periodically checking the instrument panels, swarm-visualization graphics, and video monitors.

Ethan, in a self-induced drugged sleep, became unconscious after a quick series of gasps and died a few minutes later. The session scored four on a scale of ten. A score of ten meant that the swarm carried out the attack without any correcting signals from sources external to the three sub-swarms. Ten was required to ship a swarm to the CIA. Mathis was willing to ship a trained swarm with a score of nine and take the risk of failure. With a score below nine, he knew he couldn't deliver the weapon system.

He retrieved the partially coevolved Mission Control and ComLink sub-swarms from Ethan's cell and combined them with a new Assassin sub-swarm. He then went to Wilson's cell. Wilson, asleep at first, awoke during the training. During his last moments of consciousness, Wilson had a look of horror on his face – a look Mathis would never forget. But thanks to Wilson's sacrifice, the score was now six.

Mathis found Daryl staring out of the window of his cell and pointing at his empty water bottle. Motioning for Daryl to sit down, he held up five fingers to indicate that he would be back in five minutes. Seconds later, he released the swarm from the injection chamber and began to monitor the session.

Daryl, who struggled desperately at first, was unconscious in three minutes and brain dead in just over five minutes. The irony amused Mathis. He had held up five fingers and it took five minutes. Unfortunately, the score printed out by the computer was only eight.

He would need to locate another human subject. Mathis then got a cart, took the three bodies to the primate section of the veterinary unit, and disposed of them in the large animal crematorium.

Movement on the monitor plus the sound of Graves and Stallcup shouting at each other interrupted Mathis's thoughts. Two escorts with an elderly man standing between them stood at the ramp to the primate lab. Mathis rushed to the lab and opened the large doors. The visitor introduced himself as Dr. R. T. Clement a consultant in primate biology with the San Diego Zoo. His papers and clearances checked out. Mathis greeted Dr. Clement and escorted him to his quarters.

Mathis was glad this was Friday and he could get some time away from the lab. Next week he would have to face the hostile Graves again. At least Dr. Clement could testify that the animals in the lab were properly cared for. Graves was furious when he saw their cages.

Friday at 11 pm, Mathis headed to his quarters for a weekend free of this mess.

At eight the next Monday morning, Colonel Graves banged his office door open and walked in to take charge. A gray-haired visitor sat in front of his desk.

"What are you doing here?" he said.

The visitor said nothing. Graves hurried out to his receptionist's desk.

"What's going on Ms. Jamison? Who is this guy? I didn't have any visitors scheduled."

"That's what I thought, but his appointment is in the computer for eight," she replied. Graves looked over her shoulder. Sure enough, Dr. R. T. Clement, CFO, California Microrobotic Sensor Systems, appeared on his calendar with an impressive list of security clearances.

Graves calmed himself, re-entered his office, and sat down.

"OK, Dr. Clement, what's this all about? Who's your host?"

"My host is Dr. Mathis. Among other things, my company provides tools for studying primates in the wild.

"I see you're cleared to discuss the work of Mathis and his team, so tell me your concerns. You should be aware that this project was launched by President Tannenbaum himself.

"I understand that Tannenbaum is involved. I was invited by Mathis to address concerns about the care of your large primates, but I have other ethical concerns. I want to show you a video of an experiment done by Mathis. Call up your browser, and go to the primate lab research site."

Soon Graves watched as experimental swarms with Mathis at the controls killed three men in succession. He stared in silence, listening to Clement's calm explanation of the horrific experiments.

Graves spoke after almost a minute of silence. "Dr. Clement, these video records have digital certificates that authenticate them as ours. I'll have to find out exactly how you ended up having access to them. But first I must take the appropriate action."

Graves walked to the door and spoke to Ms. Jamison, "Call the Silverbell Army Heliport and get three or four MPs out here at once." He then turned to Clement.

"Dr. Clement, you must remain here at our facilities while those who committed this crime are put under arrest. In a few hours I'll give you details on these constraints. Would you like to sit in our library while you wait?" he asked.

"That would be the perfect place for me," Clement replied.

"Good. I'll have Ms. Jamison escort you."

Clement handed Graves his business card. On it was the name and address of his company and the URL of their website. The card listed two names: R. T.

Clement, CFO, and F. P. Valentinus, CEO. Graves put the card in his pocket.

Later that day, with Mathis taken into custody and Clement gone, Graves sat down at his computer and typed the CMSS link into his browser. An attractive website appeared. The company advertised only one product:

"Keep track of your infant or toddler, anytime, anywhere, with a CMSS sensor system. Shaped as attractive mugs, our baby monitors start at only $40."

The basic mug, the forty-dollar model, had no handle and was 4 inches tall; it tapered from 3.5 inches in diameter at the top to 2.5 inches at the bottom. Four colors were available: white, tan, brown, and black. For ten dollars more, one could buy the Special Edition Mug, which had a handle and a CMSS logo.

Graves stared at the CMSS homepage in disbelief. "Why was Mathis consulting with a primate expert who also manufactured baby products?".

10 MARY MATHIS

December 31, 2141

Mary Mathis and her son Todd sat near the fireplace in their Prospect Park home at 10 p.m. on New Year's Eve. Her husband Jim, originally scheduled to arrive early afternoon from Tucson, was late.

Having spent the evening at their neighborhood Fire and Ice Festival, Todd was excited from horse-drawn hayrides, ice skating, and too much sugary hot cider. He had expected his dad to go to the festival with him, but such disappointments were now the rule rather than the exception in Todd's relationship with his father.

Jim had almost become a stranger to Mary. He began his career as an assistant professor in the Department of Electrical and Computer Engineering at the University of Minnesota. They bought their present home shortly after they arrived in Minneapolis. Mary loved the neighborhood, with its magnificent trees and friendly, politically active neighbors. The city of Minneapolis, with its cultural life and opportunities for children, was perfect for them. An advantage, not fully appreciated when they bought their home, was that Jim could walk to work -- a real convenience in the icy winters of Minnesota.

Life was great for them until five years ago when Jim, then just promoted to full professor, left his academic job to work on a secret government project located in Arizona, west of Tucson. Mary moved with Todd to Tucson for the first year of Jim's government project, but she missed her friends and medical practice in Minneapolis. She even missed the winters. Living in Tucson, they saw Jim infrequently. Seeking the comfort of familiar surroundings, Mary and Todd returned to their home in Prospect Park. Jim accepted this change without objection; in fact, he seemed relieved.

Recently, thanks to a product she purchased from CMSS, Mary and Todd could watch Jim at work. She felt guilty about spying on her husband, but allowing Todd to see his dad helped heal the family's separation wounds. The CMSS mug was a godsend for her. For the moment, the mug was out of sight behind the large schefflera in the living room. She knew she should tell Jim about it but didn't want it to be the first thing they discussed. The trick would be to tell him before Todd did.

Mary removed Todd's toys from the living room and prepared some hot cider for toasting the New Year. When she heard footsteps on the porch she ran to the door, opened it, and saw before her an exhausted man.

"Sorry I'm late, Mary," Jim said, handing her his coat. "Is Todd asleep?" They hugged each other mechanically.

"Yes, he wanted to stay up to meet you but he was exhausted. He's very tired from the festival at Luxton Park."

"Do I smell hot cider?" Jim asked, trying to change the subject from the festivities he had missed.

"Yes you do! Sit down and I'll get some."

They sat in silence for several minutes, staring at the fire. Finally, Mary said, "You look tired and overworked, Jim."

"I'm in a hell of a mess. I've invested five years on this project. This classified work has screwed up my academic career forever. We've achieved amazing things, but I can only talk about them with a few people. We haven't yet reached our final goal. Lately, everything seems to be going wrong, mostly just little things; lost data and unexpected trivial errors occur way too often."

"You knew you were risking your career when you took on this project. You laid out the potential problems very clearly to me. Do you remember?"

"Yeah, you don't need to remind me. I didn't understand the vicious politics associated with this type of project. It corrupts all who work on it, including me."

"I wish you would talk to me about it," she said.

"You wouldn't want to know," he replied, almost to himself.

The hidden mug sounded a sequence of three beeps. Jim stood up so fast that he spilled cider on his shirt. He looked as if he'd seen a ghost.

"What was that?" he asked in a whisper.

"Just my kitchen timer," Mary said, obviously lying. She knew that the beeping was in reference to Todd. He was having nightmares, or he was no longer asleep.

"Timer my ass," said Jim. "I know that sound. Don't tell me you have one of those damned things."

At that moment, a sleepy Todd appeared in his pajamas. He saw his dad and ran to him with his arms out. Jim's frown turned to a smile as he scooped his son into his arms.

"Did you bring any animals?" Todd asked, clinging to his dad with all of his might.

Mary retreated to the kitchen as fast as she could without breaking into a run.

"Animals?" Jim said, sitting down with his son in his lap.

"The monkeys and chimps you play with at your work," Todd said, in all innocence.

It took only a few seconds for Jim to connect this revelation with the beep he had just heard. He held Todd's arm so tightly that the boy squirmed to get away.

"Mary, get in here," Jim yelled. Todd, having freed himself, took off for the security of his mother. "You've been spying on us with a CMSS monitor. Show me where it is, immediately."

Jim stood and started toward his wife. Mary, now not hesitating to run, dashed over to the potted plant, lifted up the mug, and held it out at arm's length to Jim. She was visibly afraid of him.

"Please don't break it. It's been a great help to me."

"I won't break it," Jim said, holding the mug as if it were a viper. "But I can't let you keep it. This thing's a dangerous invention of a company we can't trust. You've no Idea how much trouble you could be in for spying on the lab.

"We missed you, Jim. We discovered almost by accident that we could watch you at work. Todd is very proud of you because you work with animals."

"I kill the animals. They're part of the experiments we do."

Mary held Todd close to her. This information would be upsetting, perhaps incomprehensible to him.

"I don't understand," she said.

"I can't explain. I'll have to report this security breach to the colonel in charge of our project; at some point, he'll have to tell the FBI."

"Will they arrest me?" Mary asked, with fear in her voice.

Jim thought for a moment.

"I'll tell them you discovered that this thing could penetrate our security for the first time recently. It was an accident, and you told me immediately. I'll tell them you know nothing about our work."

Mary had more immediate concerns than concocting a story.

"Will you take my mug?"

"If I take it, CMSS will get another sensor to you almost immediately. But it'll help our case if I confiscate this particular one."

Mary was pleased she would get another mug soon, but she was afraid to let Jim know.

Jim placed the mug on the coffee table and continued his explanation. "The NTIA, a government agency that reports directly to President Tannenbaum, is setting the rules for us in dealing with CMSS. We've discovered in the last few weeks that mugs outside our lab can spy on us. There must be CMSS sensors in our lab but no one has been able to locate them. It's an insidious technology that has to be stopped."

"Maybe it's from outer space!" Todd cried.

"Time for bed, Todd," Mary said, taking hold of him by his arm. "It's past midnight. You've been watching too much outer space stuff on you computer."

As Mary marched Todd out of the room, Jim sat down from exhaustion. He looked at the mug sitting on the coffee table next to his chair.

"Are you from outer space?" he asked. It gave no response.

It took Mary almost twenty minutes to get Todd calmed down. When she returned to the living room, Jim still sat staring at the mug. She sat down on the living room sofa.

""Happy New Year, Jim." She hung back. He looked unapproachable.

"Todd has been thinking just about everything is from outer space these days. It's very hard for me alone to keep control of what he watches," she said.

"Don't apologize," Jim replied, in a voice that was barely audible. "None of us thought of that."

"Can you tell me anything about what's going on at work, Jim? You look very stressed and it might help to talk about it."

"I killed three men."

Mary looked at him in disbelief.

"I can't believe you would kill anyone. What ever happened? Was it self defense? Does anyone else know about this?"

"In a strange way, I was given a promotion for it. The new colonel who temporarily had me arrested in early December was removed from his job and forced to retire. I hated the guy, so it didn't bother me. The colonel who replaced him, a tough bastard from Army Intelligence, said they'd cover up the murders because our experiments are so important to national security. Someone, most likely a government hit man, assassinated the retired guy, Graves, a few weeks ago."

The mug beeped. Text appeared on the display, projected onto the coffee table.

We copied Colonel Graves prior to his death.

"Good God, Mary," Jim said. "Maybe Todd's right. In any case, this isn't known technology. We've never heard of a mug making such a statement."

"What are we going to do?" Mary asked, in total confusion.

"I'll return Wednesday to Arizona, take this mug with me, and tell our commanding officer that it showed you images inside our lab. I cancelled my December 30 flight due to problems in the animal lab. We'll say you checked on me that day and saw me working with the animals. But you only saw me for a few minutes, around 9 a.m."

"What about the mug?" Mary asked. "Will it contradict us?"

"This mug will probably play dead, like the ones we try to reverse engineer. Even so, the military guys will be satisfied that I've taken it from you."

"This mug has already done one very odd thing, making statements about copying people," Mary said. "What does that mean? I hope you're right about it going dead like the others."

"It's a chance we'll have to take. I've been trying for weeks to get our intelligence people to go after the upper management of CMSS. I had a very strange encounter with one of them, Mr. Clement, a primate expert who consulted with our lab. He, or someone, penetrated our computer security and recorded stuff they never should have seen. They're very advanced in their technical skills in communications technology. Now I'm starting to understand why."

"You mean outer space?"

"It's possible, but it seems absurd … far-fetched. I'm obviously not going to mention outer space to the intelligence people. They'd think I'm crazy. I'm going to get the FBI to go after CMSS full force. That way maybe we can get to the bottom of this."

"What could they arrest them for? Everyone we know has a CMSS sensor. Ours has been a big help to Todd and me."

"They'll think of reasons to haul them in. That's one thing they do very well. Security violations will be just a starter. I'll tell them to give these guys physical exams right off. The intelligence guys won't think of asking me why. That will reveal such things as biotic enhancements." And it would reveal outer space connections, he thought, with a sense of embarrassment.

The thought of the FBI arresting the CMSS managers filled Mary with sadness. Tannenbaum's government would intern them for years without explanation. She wanted to know more about the three men Jim killed. Her new sensor when it arrived might reveal the reasons, but should she ask?

11 THE FBI RAID

January 13, 2142

Winter quarter had just begun. Matthew had only one course to teach, the first quarter of a graduate course in advanced seismology. He sat alone in his office at 8 a.m. on a Saturday morning, preparing for his Monday lecture on continuum mechanics. Yesterday, during his first lecture, he screwed up badly on some calculations -- no way to start the course. This time he would be over-prepared.

He found his new relationship with Laura exciting and distracting. She had jarred him out of his comfortable routine of teaching, research and surfing. It was fortunate that he could share the worrisome complexities of CMSS with her.

For the last few weeks, he had neglected his lab. Fortunately, his only graduate research student, Nancy Chen, was smart and independent. He had the time and energy to supervise another Ph.D. student, but he had better do a decent job on his lectures if he wanted to recruit one.

He looked down at his stack of old notes on continuum mechanics. Note taking hadn't been one of his strong points as a graduate student; these notes, in particular, were a mess. Perhaps a doughnut and some coffee would clarify his thinking. He grabbed a few pages and started for the door.

As he stepped out of his office, Laura called. "Guns pointed at their backs hands tied behind them. There must be fifty men surrounding the building. What a mess!"

"What are you talking about? Calm down," Matthew said.

"The FBI is at CMSS. They're arresting Clement and Valentinus and hauling away the equipment. The diorite colony display is showing me the scene real time. Mike Trent, the engineer from Boulder, is standing outside the apartment door. He phoned a few minutes ago and said he had to see us. Now the display has disappeared. You'd better get here right away."

Laura opened the door and Mike entered looking awkward and embarrassed.

"I apologize, Laura, but you and Matthew have to get over to CMSS right away. I've explained to the FBI that you two know nothing of technical importance about the sensors, but they may want you for questioning. They want me to take you there."

"Have some coffee while we wait for Matthew to get here and for me to get ready," she said.

Mike sat down at the dining room table, picked up the diorite colony, turned it over a few times, and placed it back down.

"Aren't you concerned that this rock will scratch your table?" he said, rubbing gently with his hand near the diorite.

"That's Matthew's fault for putting it there," Laura said, with mock disgust. She picked up the colony and moved it to the kitchen. By the time she was ready, Matthew was home and sitting at the table with Mike.

"Why now?" Matthew asked.

"Something happened that really pissed off some big shots," Mike said. "All hell has broken loose. I'm supposed to bring you two to the factory in case you're needed to answer questions."

"Why don't Laura and I just take my car and follow you?"

"OK. Although that's not exactly what I was told to do."

Soon they were driving to the CMSS building, following Mike's car.

Matthew was shocked by what he saw. Two vans marked FBI sat in the CMSS parking lot with armed men surrounding them. The FBI had backed a large truck up to the loading dock and were loading a metal cabinet into it. Cabinets like this one were where CMSS supposedly kept the "finished mugs."

Sam Denton, the amiable FBI agent from San Diego, approached Matthew and

Laura as soon as they got out of the car.

"Hello again, Matthew," he said. "Sometime in the next two weeks you and Laura will be questioned under oath about your experiences with CMSS. Don't disappear on us; we'll know how to find you. As for now, hang around here in case we have some questions about the stuff we're finding in the building."

"Where are Clement and Valentinus?" Matthew asked.

"They're one each in the vans. They'll be kept apart so they can't communicate with each other until they're under government confinement."

Sam offered an explanation. "Keeping the detainees separate is standard practice. The interrogators will tell each man that the other has ratted on him. That'll cause them to lose confidence in their companions and come clean."

"Come clean about what?" Laura asked. "What are they being charged with?"

"They're being turned over to the military as enemy combatants -- direct orders from President Tannenbaum," Mike volunteered.

"The 'enemy combatant' designation will allow them to be held several years for military interrogation," Sam said. "That's more effective than civilian interrogation."

"But what have they done wrong?" Laura asked.

"They've manufactured and sold equipment that's been used to spy on some of the most secret projects being undertaken by the DOD," Sam replied. "Their products have also been used for many tasteless violations of privacy. President Tannenbaum himself has been a frequent victim."

"So why haven't Matthew and I been arrested?" Laura asked.

Matthew gave her a look of exasperation. Fortunately, Agent Denton wasn't paying any attention to her. He was walking away from them to help clear a path for the vans containing the newly acquired detainees. Mike, still standing beside them, answered Laura's question."

"They searched Matthew's apartment and didn't find anything from CMSS. They didn't search Laura's apartment, so don't encourage them. I assured them that you were both technically ignorant of the company's devices, and your only role was advice on marketing."

"Suppose they'd found a mug in my apartment? What would they have done?" Matthew asked.

"Nothing for now, but President Tannenbaum has been meeting with his closest advisors and discussing the possibility of rounding up all CMSS customers," Mike replied.

"That's crazy," Matthew said, amazed by the stupidity of Tannenbaum. "These are mostly parents with children at this point. What's he going to do, provide babysitters for them while they're in jail? This will create a publicity nightmare for the government."

"That concern is why he's hesitating," Mike continued. "By the way, I haven't told anyone about your comment that these things are augmented by a wide array of additional sensors. I'm still hoping you can come in with us on our business venture. Maybe we'll have time to talk in private when things calm down. We need to transform this same technology into something exclusively for use by the DOD."

Matthew noticed some rocks and bricks piled against the side of the now empty building and wondered if some of them might be colonies, shape transformed so they wouldn't be taken by the FBI?

Laura had been staring at a row of corvids that sat on a fence overlooking the raid: some crows, some ravens, and a couple of very large jays. She nudged Matthew to get his attention.

"Look at those birds, Matthew. Someone has drugged or poisoned them. They don't look right."

"How can you think of something like that at a time like this?" Matthew said.

Laura continued to stare. Then she started to laugh.

Matthew felt sorry for the enthusiastic Sam Denton who had now assumed a role of importance in directing the vans out of the parking lot. If Denton thought that his association with this event was going to get him promoted, he was probably mistaken. He heard Denton call out to the agent in charge of transporting the prisoners, "Get word to Colonel Stallcup that they should be given physical exams as soon as they get to Camp Sigma. Check for biotic enhancement."

Matthew was certain that the humanoid colonies had some reason for allowing the FBI to arrest them. The worst thing the FBI could possibly do, in terms of protecting government secrets, would be to take the Valentinus and Clement colonies deeper into the government's world of prison camps and classified information.

Sam Denton and some other FBI agents were motioning for a small group curious onlookers to leave. The truck, now pulling away from the loading dock, contained all of the confiscated equipment.

Mike was now off in the distance talking to the TV news crews while Denton was absorbed in his role as FBI advisor to the raid. Matthew decided that he and Laura should leave immediately. Denton knew where to find them if he needed them.

They drove in silence until they were several miles from the factory. As the road leveled out along the coast with the comforting power of the ocean clearly in view, Laura broke the silence.

"I am pretty sure that the crows and ravens that I thought were drugged are actually colonies. I bet you didn't notice."

Matthew wished she would stop pointing out all the things he didn't notice.

"Right, I *didn't* notice. I was pretty sure that the mugs they confiscated aren't colonies of microbots."

"Another thing that's weird is how does Mike, a low level government engineer, know about President Tannenbaum's discussions with his advisors? How does he know that Tannenbaum is thinking about rounding up all owners of CMSS products?" Laura asked.

Mike Trent did have several mugs for reverse engineering. But the mugs, by his own admission, weren't functioning properly. Matthew had an idea.

"Suppose one of Mike's friends bought a mug, and Tannenbaum is a threat to that person's child. Mike may be learning things about Tannenbaum indirectly from the friend."

"Way too complicated," Laura said. "Maybe Tannenbaum is a threat to everyone so anyone who has a mug could observe his activities."

Matthew again felt a bit irritated. Her suggestion was a brilliant one.

12 CAMP SIGMA

February 2142

First Lieutenant Sean Penrose sat in a small underground office in the Chiricahua Mountains of Southeastern Arizona. He had just finished reading the Revised Bush Guidelines for torture which defined torture as follows:

"Torture is the act of causing a person to experience, without causing death, intense pain to the point where the suffering is of the kind that is equivalent to the pain that would be associated with serious physical injury so severe that death, organ failure, or permanent damage resulting in a loss of significant body function will likely result."

He had to read the statement several times. "I think I understand what this is saying, Captain Taylor," he said. "But how does this relate to the building of Camp Sigma?"

"Too many senior citizens couldn't survive interrogation when the Revised Bush Guidelines were used to define the outer limits of physical abuse," Captain Taylor replied. "President Tannenbaum ordered the construction of Camp Sigma to deal with this problem. This camp is for the specific purpose of confining and interrogating seniors who are a risk to our country."

Sean shook his head in disbelief. Captain Ashley Taylor was temporary commanding officer of Camp Sigma's Joint Detention Group (JDG). She was possibly in serious legal trouble. Sean read the national news regularly. He'd never seen anything about senior citizens dying from interrogation. Of course, the government would classify any such deaths as secret. His dad was a senior and a very tough one, but he had a bad memory. Maybe that was also a factor in the deaths. Some seniors couldn't come up with the answers even if their lives depended on it or couldn't even remember the questions.

"These guidelines are vague and poorly worded," Sean said. "I see why they might be problematic for seniors, Captain Taylor. For an old person, organ failure might come sooner than for a young person. Even a loud noise or trying to jump out of the way of a jogger or bike might do it."

"Exactly. Our guidelines here are different from those at the regular interrogation camps. We've returned to the older DOD three-category guidelines. The government has modified even those interrogation procedures for our seniors. You can call me Ashley if you wish."

"This is an intimidating place, Ashley. To get to this room, I went through four sets of double-caged doors guarded by angry MP's."

"Camp Sigma is the latest class ten prison camp. It's got all of the new technology; an escape would be impossible." She added that last remark by habit and suddenly felt foolish.

"I guess we might say *almost* impossible," Sean said. "That brings us to the point of my visit, your legal defense."

"You seem very young to be an Army Judge Advocate," she said. "Have you ever had a case like this before?"

"This is my first case. Right after passing the Arizona bar exams, I went straight to the Army Judge Advocate General's Corps. Just finished their training program."

Ashley looked shaken. "You don't understand. I need someone who knows what they're doing. My career, maybe my life, depends on this."

Sean stared at her in silence for a moment before speaking. "I know what I'm doing. Count on me to bust my ass on this case."

"If I've insulted you, I'm sorry," she said, realizing that he was her only hope.

"I accept your apology," Sean said without enthusiasm. "Now let's get down to business. Apparently, two old guys managed to escape from this class ten fortress. Your commander has accused you of aiding them. What's your story?"

I did nothing to aid them," she began, "but I was the last one to visit them in their solitary confinement cells. That makes me the fall guy."

"Who are these guys who escaped? When were they admitted to Camp Sigma?"

"There were two of them, both admitted on the evening of Saturday, January 20. They were from a private company, California Microrobotic Sensor Systems, that made baby monitors. They had violated some sort of rules concerning communications technology."

 "Baby monitors?" Sean repeated in disbelief.

"Their names are, Mr. Valentinus and Mr. Clement, and they are the principal executives of the company."

Sean put down his pen and paper. Maybe this shouldn't be his first case. "Why would these guys be put in Camp Sigma? This is no place for white-collar criminals. Tannenbaum doesn't care about them," he said.

Ashley was silent for a moment, thoughtful.

"I don't know why they were sent here, but there are others here who are even less likely candidates for high security interrogation. The government works that way. They're being super cautious. That's also why they keep people here so long. No one wants to be responsible for releasing someone who might cause trouble later."

This whole business of government camps was frightening to Sean. In a strange way it made him glad he was in JAG Corps; maybe he could make some changes from within.

"What did the CMSS detainees do to get solitary confinement?"

"It's standard procedure for seniors," Ashley replied. "They all go to solitary for the first three weeks they're here. In about half the cases, that's enough to get them to talk without any formal interrogation. Isolation is a Category II counter-resistance technique, allowed under our senior guidelines."

"I've heard some horrible rumors about solitary confinement in our government's detention centers," Sean said

"Our seniors are isolated under much more humane conditions than those used in the regular centers. Each of our solitary cells has a metal-frame bed of excellent quality, the same type of bed used in our hospital. There's a toilet in one corner of the room and a washbasin in one of the others. The basic restriction is that our detainees can have no personal items or reading material for the duration of their isolation. Their cells are dimly lit but not completely dark."

"So these CMSS guys went into isolation from the moment they arrived. Don't cameras watch them the whole time? If so, that should be enough to clear you. We could see how they got out and who helped them."

"There are high tech cameras, but something seems to have gone wrong with them. Gaps occurred," Ashley confessed.

That was bad news Sean noted. It would make Ashley's case much more difficult for him. He needed more details.

"We may have some problems ahead for us, Ashley. Tell me about the times you visited those guys' cells and about any procedural irregularities, however slight, that you or anyone else committed in dealing with them."

"I only visited their cells once. Three irregularities have occurred that I know about, two before my visit with them, the third after."

"Take them in order," Sean said. "Give me all the details."

"Well -- this is embarrassing to me -- the evening the two men arrived here I got an email, sent to me at home. It was from my former commander at Fort Huachuca asking that the CMSS detainees be given regular physical exercise starting at admission date. That's allowed only after the solitary confinement phase." She handed Sean a copy of the email.

The email was from a Colonel Stallcup. It was short, "CMSS guys must get reg. phys. exs. at adm."

"So what's embarrassing about this? Why does he think they need to get exercise?" Sean asked.

"Stallcup was once a senior advisor to Camp Sigma but is not directly involved with us anymore. As such, he shouldn't comment on particular prisoners. Colonel Stallcup, above all, should know this." She hesitated and added, "I shouldn't have mentioned this to you."

 "I'm your lawyer. I need to know such things. I still don't see why this email should be a problem for us."

"Under our rules, I'm supposed to reveal any such note to my superiors. I didn't do that. Stallcup and I were close friends at Fort Huachuca."

Warning signals went off for Sean.

"So, you were trying to protect Stallcup at the risk of your career. How close to him were you? Sorry to ask, but that's something I need to know."

"Very close. We were lovers." Ashley's face had become as red as her hair.

Sean paused to let her regain her composure. He looked again at the email.

"Are you sure this refers to physical exercise? Maybe Stallcup meant physical exams at admission, like the doctors checking them over." Sean hated the lazy habit of abbreviations, a habit prevalent in the military. Ashley looked surprised.

"I guess it could mean that. We do give them physical exams at the end of solitary confinement, before interrogation starts. Stallcup would know that."

"Maybe, for some reason, these particular men should have had physical exams at the start of solitary," Sean conjectured. "We'll never know because we'd be fools to call Stallcup to testify. So much for the first irregularity. What's the second?"

"The second involves the dog. Solitary confinement for seniors is not entirely solitary. We stop by their cells at least once a day for a few minutes to make contact, to give them a hint of things to follow. The linguists will chat with them a few minutes, small talk. The MPs will bring their dogs by, enter the cell, and restrain the dogs as they try to attack the prisoners. It's just show; they don't let the dog's get close."

"So let me guess, the second irregularity is that a dog bit one of your prisoners."

"Stranger than that. An MP brought his dog into Mr. Clement's cell Monday morning, January 22. Amazingly, the dog was afraid of the prisoner. The MP became furious. He dragged his dog so close that it could have bitten Mr. Clement."

"Good," Sean said. "That's got to be a violation of some sort of rule. Continue."

Ashley leaned closer to Sean and lowered her voice.

"The video cameras show that Mr. Clement didn't move or say anything to the dog or the MP. But for some reason the dog went limp. It's a big dog and the MP had to carry it out of the cell block. His dog has never recovered. It's forgotten its training. Isn't that weird?"

"I've never heard of anything like it, but I don't know much about dogs. It's my intuition that this incident is tangential to your case and is unlikely to either help or hurt you," he replied.

"Do you want to hear about my one and only visit with the detainees?" Ashley asked

Of course! That's an important issue before us. Your case may hinge on what happened during that visit."

"I'm a trained linguist, specialty Slavic languages. But I'm also an expert in ASL, American Sign Language. These guys have not said a word since we arrested them. In a regular interrogation center, they would get the shit kicked out of them for remaining silent, but we have to be more gentle here. One of the other linguists suggested I try ASL on them."

"What the hell," Sean said. "You don't even know if they *can* speak?"

"They can speak English. We've learned that from their customers. ASL was a long shot, but it worked. I tried it on both of them, and each one responded. In keeping with regulations, our conversations were short and about trivial stuff. That was Friday afternoon, January 26."

"That's amazing," Sean said. "Perhaps they were told they had the right to remain silent and believed it. My summary of this case says they were discovered missing from their cells the next morning, Saturday January 27."

Sean, now thoroughly enjoying the mystery, continued.

"All right, now we're getting to the important part. You don't know exactly how the prisoners got out, but tell me what you do know. You also need to tell me the third irregularity. Your visit to their cells as a linguist was a part of your job, not an irregularity," he said.

"The third irregularity was the presence of storage trunks in their cells. Remember, we don't allow personal effects of any sort in the cells. Each of the CMSS detainees had a large empty storage trunk under his bed. We discovered this fact after the men escaped. This is not just a small irregularity;

this is a *huge* irregularity."

"Certainly they can't blame you for this violation, Ashley. Besides, the cell cameras must have recorded the presence of the trunks. More amazing is how such trunks could get past all of these MPs."

"My best guess," Ashley continued, "is that some accomplice put them there before the prisoners were brought to their cells. Once per week the MPs do a thorough inspection of the interior of the cells. Video cameras record that an inspection was done on January 23 and showed the guard looking under the beds. He claims he saw nothing. The cells are poorly lit, and the trunks were made from a heavy black plastic. I suppose he could have looked right at them and not seen anything."

Sean was hopeful.

"These trunks, Ashley, are the key to getting you cleared. We need to show that you had nothing to do with them. If they are heavy, you couldn't have gotten them to the cells without help. We need to trace them to see who manufactured them and who purchased them. Where are they now?"

"Tuesday morning, January 30, the trunks were hauled to a storage facility above ground in the general maintenance area for Camp Sigma," Ashley answered.

Sean now had an opportunity to get others involved, people outside the closed world of the detention center. Energized, he sat on the edge of his chair.

"Great. I'll get permission to inspect them and bring some experts with me. Who do I contact here to make arrangements?" he asked.

"That would be the Army Corps of Engineers representative assigned to our project. But the MPs told me the trunks are missing. They've been stolen."

With this news, Sean slumped back in his chair, his hand rubbing his eyes. He felt a headache coming on.

"Man, that's bad news for us! How in the hell could that happen?"

Ashley, obviously fascinated by the mystery, waved her hand in the direction of the camp's general maintenance area.

"The outside area is pretty secure but nothing like down here. Still, it's amazing that anyone could steal such large items."

Sean had no regrets about joining the U.S. Army JAG Corps. Would his other cases be this challenging?

"I need to think about all of this, Ashley. My gut feeling is that the folks who are key to this are the ones who moved those trunks to the maintenance area. I think you're going to get off with no stain on your record. But that's only lawyer's intuition. Let's meet again in one week, same time and place."

"Thank you Sean," Ashley said, with a big smile that made her look radiant. "I'm looking forward to seeing you next Thursday the 22nd. Maybe we'll know more about all of this by then."

Sean worked his way past the MP's, checked through the main gate, and climbed into his car. He felt a profound sense of relief to be out. The whole place was repressive, bordering on lunacy. About half a mile from Camp Sigma, he pulled his car over to the side of the road, got out and stood for a moment in the cool evening air looking back.

A large fence of iron bars, topped with coiled barbed wire, surrounded the outer perimeter of the camp. There was a guard tower every twenty yards. Searchlights swung back and forth, covering the grounds in a seemingly random pattern. Guards stood at the main gate night and day. How could anyone, especially senior citizens, escape?

Three very unusual events happened in connection with the detention of the CMSS prisoners: The morning of January 27 the two CMSS prisoners were missing from their cells and have not been found; against regulations, a large black empty trunk was in each man's cell; after being hauled to the above ground storage facility, the trunks have not been found. It was a miracle that any one of these events took place without detection, let alone all of them.

Sean looked again at the layout of the detention center. The most likely possibility was that the movements of the men and trunks were somehow bundled into the fewest possible challenges to the security structure of the camp. That would mean that the two trunks and the men came in by the same method, at the same time or nearly so, and the men, together with the trunks, were removed from the maintenance area at roughly the same time; perhaps with the men in the trunks. However, word of the discovery of the trunks had gotten around. That would make them risky containers for the escaping men.

Stumped, he got back in the car and drove off. Fifty miles north as he drove along a level stretch he saw someone hitchhiking on the side of the road. He was not supposed to pick up hitchhikers in his government car, but this guy was elderly and wasn't wearing a coat. He would freeze to death during the night. He pulled over and stopped. As the old man got into the front seat another old guy dressed the same way came out of the bushes and got into the back seat. They were cordial and looked harmless. "Where are you guys going?" Sean asked.

"Santa Fe," said the guy in the front seat. "We're in ceramics," said the guy in the back seat.

13 CHAOS, ADJUSTMENT AND A NEW MISSION

January 2250

In the second half of the twenty-second century, when the great proliferation of CMSS monitors occurred, human culture descended into a time of chaos. The economy of the time depended largely on hype, if not outright deception. The microbots took all of this in stride. They had observed that humans, stressed by climate change and overcrowding, were following demagogues and succumbing to unscientific fads. They predicted immanent extinction of the human race unless something was done. Their standard policy for such problems dictated that they create an environment where all humans could get accurate information from a reliable source, namely CMSS.

The period from 2150 to 2190 was the most chaotic. The microbots dropped all pretense of non-interference. Some militias attempted to confiscate monitors from everyone in their territory. They were unsuccessful. Small groups of humans tried to go underground and erect shielding to protect themselves from observation. The microbots monitored them but otherwise ignored them. Anyone, anywhere, anytime could follow the daily activities of world leaders. Attempts by nation states to restrict sensor use failed. A world of "symmetric information" ensued. Cultures and individuals who couldn't tolerate the reality of others disagreeing with them became violent, killing many innocent people. To the surprise of most doomsayers, however, by the end of the twenty-second century the human race came to a new equilibrium. Once human-based microbots in the colonies attained a certain level of influence, it was possible to adopt a privacy policy compatible with human sensitivities.

People everywhere wanted the microbots to make virtual copies of them – they viewed this as a form of immortality. The ultimate honor was to become a core persona for a microbot..

In December of 2249 all microbots received word that volunteers would be needed for a new and important mission. The microbots in the Clement colony decided to participate as a unit.

Laura-bot and her friends, members of the Clement colony, gathered in one of the control chambers to discuss the adventure that awaited them. She had been appointed to lead the discussion.

"Our colony will leave the solar system and head outward towards the edge of the galaxy," she announced. "The goal is to be in a position where we can start recording early signs of the eventual collision of the Andromeda Galaxy with the Milky Way. The first faint signals from natural history colonies in the Andromeda Galaxy might be picked up in as early as two billion years from now. If so, we will start exchanging records with them about that time. We expect that they will also be sending expeditions to the edge of their galaxy to contact us.

J.P. Graves-bot was struck by the magnitude and daring of the project. "Nothing like thinking ahead," he said.

They would find many fascinating worlds to visit and much natural history to record and share with other natural history colonies on their way to the outer reaches of the Milky Way. But the human-based microbots knew that by going on this mission they would never be on the surface of the earth again. This realization gave them cause for reflection. There were special times in the early evening, when the air was still, that the human based microbots would set their clock speeds to coincide with earth time and transmit the experience of biological life going through its preparations for the coming night to their core personae. These special occasions, enjoyed equally by the microbots and their human hosts, would be lost to them forever. "Although these moments could be simulated," Laura-bot once commented, "it's knowing that we are observing real biological events taking place on our home planet that makes them so special."

"How are we supposed to travel?" Matthew-bot asked.

"We will transform Clement into a spaceship," Laura-bot replied.

"In Camp Sigma we transformed him into a box in just four hours," J.P. Graves-bot said. "I suppose we can transform him into a spaceship in four months.

14 REFLECTIONS OF MATTHEW-BOT AND LAURA-BOT

May 2250

The Clement based microbots were heading out of the inner solar system in their spaceship fashioned from a restructured Clement. Matthew-bot and Laura-bot were linked together to simulate past experiences and discuss the future. By slowing their clock speeds the microbots could shorten the perceived time of the voyage. The biological Matthew and Laura were deceased.

"It's a shame Laura's aunt Amanda couldn't be a core persona," Matthew-bot said. "A core persona has to be copied from a living human."

"Don't worry about her, virtual Amanda is somewhere in the outer solar system taking charge of the situation," Laura-bot said. "But where? I could never get an answer from Clement."

"I once got some hints from the 47 Ursae Majoris guys," Matthew-bot said. "Basically the microbots don't know where Laura's mote civilization is located. The general pattern for these new civilizations is that they either disappear or soon come back to take vengeance on their creators. This danger is why Clement and Valentinus were so concerned about the biological Laura. They view her with reverence as a creator of a new civilization."

"I guess many of these new civilizations evolve rapidly and get interested in their own virtual worlds to the point where they lose interest in the actual universe," Laura-bot said. "Fortunately, not all of them lose interest!"

Mathew-bot had concluded that the "actual universe" might itself be a simulated universe, but Laura-bot had no patience with that point of view.

"We will have many new things to learn when the Milky Way and Andromeda galaxies merge," Matthew-bot said. "But what about the billions of galaxies that aren't gravitationally bound to us. We will never know what is going on there."

"Relax, you just can't know everything," Laura-bot replied.

Mathew-bot realized that there was a certain futility to their efforts.

"You know," he said, "We are very lucky to exist at a time in the history of our universe when we are able to see back to its beginning. What are the chances of that?"

"The question isn't well defined, but probably just about zero," Laura-bot replied.

"That sort of bothers me," Matthew-bot replied. "Why are we so lucky? Eventually, none of the newly evolving civilizations in our merged galaxy will be able to see back to the beginning due to the expanding universe."

We could inform them about the big bang, but it is against our principles," Laura-bot said. "Perhaps we will have to change our principles."

"At least we have each other," Matthew-bot noted, calming down.

"Now you're getting the idea," Laura-bot replied, indicating in a definitive way that the discussion was over.

AUTHOR'S NOTES

Chapter 1: AMANDA

The Picnic, July 2060 What could go wrong with letting a tech company record your anniversary picnic? Amanda sees potential problems immediately. The rest of the guests appear to be clueless. The technology needed to create a virtual picnic and to copy the guests in a believable way (for later virtual reality sessions) will probably be available by 2060. In 2060 the full range of tactile signals for the avatars may not be fully programmed but they will feel pain. We may assume that the avatars at the picnic are self aware in a sense that allows us to feel empathy for them. Our universe is very accommodating to computers -- computers operating at speeds and using architectures far beyond what we have now are possible. Researchers at university, industrial and government labs are now developing the technology that will lead to the creation of sentient, intelligent avatars. See _Wikipedia: Virtual reality, Wikipedia: Limits of computation, Wikipedia: Neuromorphic engineering, Wikipedia: Quantum computing._

ERVS: April 2140 For motes, see _Wikipedia: Smartdust._ By 2140 ERVS has become much more advanced in its simulations. Their main product is the virtual simulation of events, picnics, weddings, sports events, etc. The avatars they create for events are generally accepted as self aware and sentient. The question of ethical treatment of the many avatars stored in the ERVS archives is of great concern to Laura. She is furious at the gamers and sets out to use the computer power of the new motes to take revenge.

Daggett: May 2140 We get a glimpse of the cruel intentions of the gamers and their abuse of the sentient avatars in immersive virtual environments. _Wikipedia:_

Virtual reality, Wikipedia: Immersion (Virtual reality). Cruelty towards avatars in computer games is standard now and excused because they don't feel pain.

Amanda Arrives: July 2140 Amanda is copied (as code) from her older representation as an avatar in the original picnic of July 2060. Her data structures (machine representations) are updated to current high standards. She is copied into a 2140 scene similar to that of the picnic of July 2060 so she won't be too badly shocked when she emerges from her hiding place under the table. She is greeted by modern sentient avatars, Kevin and Errett, as well as other avatars in the simulated welcoming environment. The computer science behind these events has been developed by Laura in her ERVS lab using (without permission) company resources.

Amanda's New Home: July 2140 Here we introduce a theme to be followed in the rest of our story: networked computers. See *Wikipedia: Computer networks.* Amanda, the intelligent human avatar copied from the original picnic and updated, can now be "brought to life" in different environments created by any sufficiently powerful computer. It turns out that the ERVS motes have become "sufficiently powerful" to bring her to life in a limited environment. Amanda's mote is about the size and shape of a water bear (*Wikipedia: Tardigrade*). Her mote has some mobility in the "real world" and can change her internal and external environment on small scales. Amanda's current environment is a casita. Each of the many avatars that welcomed Amanda earlier in the day has its own mote. These motes, in various groupings, can form themselves into networked systems capable of simulating more complex environments. Errett, Kevin and Amanda have formed a networked system of three motes. The concept of bringing an avatar of a deceased person into being in a physical structure they can control is an achievable analog of Mary Shelly's famous story Frankenstein. This version of Shelly's tale is doable and less scary.

ERVS: July 2140 We return to the lab to get Laura's and Errett's perspective on the three docking motes. The biological Laura and Errett must come to terms with the distinction between their biological selves in the "real world" and their virtual selves in the motes. Already they are losing control of their creations and the motes plus avatars are instructing each other. Worse, we learn that Laura has enhanced virtual Amanda with sufficient understanding of the ERVS system to hack into the code that links the immersion salons to the ERVS library of recorded events .

The Fourth Try, TIS: October 2140 We are back to the gamers. We learn that Amanda, using Laura's enhancements, has taken personal revenge against the gamers by attacking Daggett's avatar as it arrived at the picnic via the TIS immersion system.

The Journey Begins: January 2141 Errett (the biological guy) is sitting alone in his office on New Years Eve thinking of recent events. He is relieved that after Amanda castrated Daggett's avatar, she has settled down to less dramatic forms of revenge. Errett reveals that a spaceship carrying thousands of new motes plus their avatars and a supply of mote repair kits has escaped earth. We suppose that the occupants of these motes are copies of existing avatars, perhaps multiple copies. We are witnessing the birth of a new civilization. Errett realizes that this civilization needs a purpose difficult and interesting enough to stimulate its development. He decides that the study of the natural history of our galaxy would provide such a purpose and that the virtual Erretts on the journey would also come up with this idea. This brings us to the rest of our story.

Chapter 2: MATTHEW CASE

September 1 2141

Matthew Case, just starting his academic career at Scripps Institution of Oceanography, by chance (or was it?) picks up an interesting rock on the beach. The "rock" turns out to be a colony of microrobots (microbots) from outer space. These microbots refer to themselves as "life forms," the citizens of their civilization. They have been studying the earth's natural history for 150 million years and are dedicated to the task. As natural historians they don't want to interfere with the creatures they are studying and have kept their presence a secret since they arrived on earth. They keep records in the form of computer simulations of the organisms they study. They can also simulate humans. We should note that Errett, drunk in his office early January 1, 2141, conjectured that the study of natural history would give Laura's ERVS mote colony a uniting purpose. He also worried what would happen if the motes themselves, at that point simply mobile computers hosting virtual humans, might evolve to become sentient living beings. Apparently this is exactly what has happened in the evolution of the microbots (analogous to the motes).

For some time perspective, the earth is about 4.5 billion years old and is divided into Eons: Hadean, Archean, Proterozoic, Phanerozoic.. The Hadean plus Archean lasted about two billion years, the Proterozoic lasted about two billion years and the Phanerozoic about 0.5 billion so far. The microbots have recorded natural history for only the last 0.15 billion years. See *Wikipedia: Cretaceous, Wikipedia: Cenozoic.*

Chapter 3: LAURA STEVER

September 7, 2141

We meet Laura of Chapter 1 again. Matthew has been asked by the microbots of his rock colony to get in touch with her. Matthew and Laura were undergrads together at University of California, Berkeley. Laura listens with some skepticism to Matthew's encounter with the microbots and the rock colony. She has had a somewhat mysterious encounter herself with a strange guy whom she calls Valentinus who has an intricate knowledge of human history. "Valentinus" is also the name of a historical figure from human history. See *Wikipedia: Valentinus.* Matthew later will try to impress Laura with his knowledge of this historical figure's teachings. He fails to impress! Laura agrees to meet Matthew in the campus library and introduce him to her acquaintance Valentinus.

Chapter 4, VALENTINUS

September 10, 2141

Here we introduce another bit of technology, the android or humanlike robot. See *Wikipedia: Android (robot).* Matthew learns that Valentinus is another creation of the microbots, a humanlike robot or "android." It seems the microbots simulate humans as well as other animals they are studying. Matthew learns that the early versions of the microbots were created by a carbon-based life form over two billion years ago in a planet near a star in the Sagittarius Arm of our galaxy. Matthew is shocked to learn that the microbots destroyed their creators. See *Wikipedia: Carina-Sagittarius Arm, Wikipedia: Carbon-based life.*

Chapter 5, DINNER PARTY

September 24, 2141

Matthew is an expert in geophysics but doesn't have a wide range of knowledge. He prefers to surf, etc. Laura is a genius at computer science, theoretical and applied. She also has a wide range of interests in history and philosophy. Matthew does his best to impress her. We are introduced to

California Microrobotic Sensor Systems, CMSS, and its high level management. They sell baby monitors and nothing else. Matthew conjectures that the monitors are the way the microbots are going to increase their surveillance of humans.

Chapter 6, VIRTUAL MATTHEW

October 28, 2141

Three microbots, analogous to the three motes in Amanda's new home of July 2140, have joined together to create a complex virtual simulation. In this case, the three microbots are referred to as Marta-bot, Kaholo-bot and Laura-bot. They are simulating Hapuna beach on the Big Island in Hawaii. Like the real Hapuna beach, the simulated beach has a great shore break for virtual Matthew to bodysurf. Matthew-bot is a microbot being trained to accept and empathize with its host, virtual Matthew. Microbots would communicate with each other as computers at high speeds and using their chosen protocols. When communicating with biological or virtual humans, microbots would communicate in the appropriate human language (as Valentinus, an android in the library, communicated with the biological Matthew). We get a glimpse here of the complexity of the interaction between the microbots and their virtual hosts. This association will be long term, long after the biological life forms have disappeared. The biological Matthew does not appear here.

Chapter 7, WATCHING THE BABY

October 28, 2141

We get a disturbing comedy of errors here about what might transpire when someone is in the possession of a CMSS mug. The "acquaintance graphs" are similar in concept to the "knowledge graph" or "knowledge base" used by Google and are similarly inclined to misinterpretation. See *Wikipedia: Knowledge Graph.*

Chapter 8, OFFICIAL VISITORS AND MEETING MANGEMENT

November 20, 2041

We note that the NTIA reports to President Tannenbaum. See *Wikipedia: National Telecommunications and Information Administration.* The ITS is a part of the Department of Commerce. See *Wikipedia: Institute for Telecommunication Sciences.* The photonics systems used by the microbots are most likely using the near infrared. *Wikipedia: Photonics.* Matthew's nightmares about actual biological copies being made of him (not something that would be done in his world) reveal his anxieties about his virtual copies.

Chapter 9, SAUCEDA MOUNTAINS

December 1, 2141

Swarms of motes or smart dust used as weapons have a history in fiction and nonfiction. See *Wikipedia: Smartdust.* The Sauceda Mountains of Arizona have an interesting geological history but that is not relevant to our story. This chapter describes a classical scenario of scientists and engineers becoming corrupted by the nature of their goals. In this chapter we see how the microbots in android form, Clement in particular, might gain access to secret projects. As Valentinus explained to Matthew, "To study humans we need to have mobility, proximity, and high bandwidth communications at short range. We must mingle with them. An inconspicuous human form works best for certain special purposes."

Chapter 10, MARY MATHIS

December 31, 2141

Jim Mathis returns from his research projects in the Sauceda Mountains Research Center, SMRC, to visit his family. He was not aware that the lab visit of Dr. Clement, San Diego Zoo, had resulted in sensors and microbot colonies being placed in his lab, but he was beginning to suspect it. Learning that his laboratory work can be spied on by his wife and son sets him on the course of getting the FBI to go after CMSS.

Chapter 11, THE FBI RAID

January 13, 2142

The FBI raid instigated most likely by Jim Mathis takes place. Laura, Matthew, Mike, from ITS, and Sam from the San Diego office of the FBI are in attendance. Protocols followed for arresting human suspects are applied to sophisticated androids, including possibly telling them their right to remain silent. We learn that President Tannenbaum himself has been a victim of violations of privacy. Laura, guesses why.

Chapter 12, CAMP SIGMA

February 2142

Sean Penrose, a new Army Judge Advocate, is tasked with defending Captain Ashley Taylor, temporary commanding officer of Camp Sigma's Joint Detainee Group, because Clement and Valentinus have escaped from Camp Sigma, a government prison and interrogation camp for senior citizens. *Wikipedia: Judge Advocate. Wikipedia: Chiricahua Mountains. Wikipedia Fort Huachuca.*

Chapter 13, CHAOS, ADJUSTMENT AND A NEW MISSION

January 2250

The distance from the earth to where the microbots must be in two billion years is 30,000 light years. They are comfortable traveling at 0.01 the speed of light which would get them into position in only 3,000,000 years. They are supposed to try to contact the natural history colonies of the Andromeda Galaxy in 2 billion years. Thus, there will be plenty of time to hang out in the outer limb of the milky way and study natural history while they wait for the full collision in 4 to 4.5 billion years. *Wikipedia: Andromeda--Milky Way Collision.*

Chapter 14, REFLECTIONS OF MATTHEW-BOT AND LAURA-BOT

May 2250

There may be billions of civilizations in our galaxy in places where biological life doesn't exist. They may be interested only in their own virtual worlds. We may never know anything about them. In fact, such a civilization may now be sharing the earth with us. *Wikipedia: Simulation hypothesis.*